# An
# *Amish Courtship*
# on ICE MOUNTAIN

Center Point
Large Print

Also by Kelly Long and available from
Center Point Large Print:

*The Amish Bride of Ice Mountain*
*An Amish Man of Ice Mountain*
*The Amish Heart of Ice Mountain*

# An
# *Amish Courtship*
# on ICE MOUNTAIN

# Kelly Long

CENTER POINT LARGE PRINT
THORNDIKE, MAINE

This Center Point Large Print edition
is published in the year 2018 by arrangement with
Kensington Publishing Corp.

The text of this Large Print edition is unabridged.
In other aspects, this book may vary
from the original edition.
Printed in the United States of America
on permanent paper.
Set in 16-point Times New Roman type.

ISBN: 978-1-68324-652-7

Library of Congress Cataloging-in-Publication Data

Names: Long, Kelly, author.
Title: An Amish courtship on Ice Mountain / Kelly Long.
Description: Center Point large print edition. | Thorndike, Maine :
    Center Point Large Print, 2018. | Series: Ice Mountain |
    Series: Center Point Large Print edition romance
Identifiers: LCCN 2017046871 | ISBN 9781683246527
    (hardcover : alk. paper)
Subjects: LCSH: Amish—Fiction. | Large type books. |
    GSAFD: Love stories. | Christian fiction.
Classification: LCC PS3612.O497 A826 2018 | DDC 813/.6—dc23
LC record available at https://lccn.loc.gov/2017046871

# An
# *Amish Courtship*
## on ICE MOUNTAIN

# Prologue

Twelve-year-old Joel Umble crept forward on his hands and knees in the thick pine needles, then paused to kneel upright, extending his right palm to the big wolf caught in the steel trap. The animal had nearly chewed its front left foot off in an attempt to escape the cruel teeth of the metal and now gave a threatening growl.

"*Kumme, hund,* peace between you and me," the *buwe* murmured. "I will pray for your healing and set you free." He swallowed, never breaking his gaze from the large golden eyes that were dilated with pain and rage. Joel inched closer, praying aloud, until he'd stretched his palm and fingers to their utmost.

Savage white teeth closed with a snap, and Joel drew a thankful breath when the long muzzle and black nose lowered and he felt the brush of the animal against his skin; seeking, scenting, roughly tender . . .

The sudden report of a gun seemed to shake the ground beneath Joel's knees, and his arm was splattered by the wolf's blood. He twisted in surprise and fury as his older *bruder* Judah lowered the weapon. "Joel, you're a fool. Praying for a pelt . . . What would Fater have said?"

Joel blinked away angry tears and turned back to the dead animal, sinking his hand into the thick gray fur. "Fater did not trap," he bit out.

Joel heard Judah step closer, the pine crunching beneath his boots. "The wolf was mine and what is mine, I keep. Remember that, Joel."

"And what is *Gott*'s?"

"What He takes, little penitent." Judah laughed with open cruelty. "Now *geh* back to the cabin; I must skin the beast."

Joel got unsteadily to his feet, then walked away from the wolf as his *bruder* passed him with a hunting knife drawn.

# Chapter One

*Ice Mountain*
*March 10, 1958*

Despite the frost in the moonlit air, nineteen-year-old Martha Yoder wanted a bath in the creek. She grew tired, every so often, of cramming herself into the tiny hip tub her family used all winter. She gathered towels and a clean *nacht*gown and slipped out of the cabin before anyone might notice she was gone. The moon cast a halo of light on the surface of the deep snow as she plowed her way to the small shed where tools were kept. She wanted an ax, in case part of the creek had frozen over a bit.

She whistled as she made her way along the moonlit path, the sound comforting in the still of the *nacht*—not that she needed any solace to be alone. Caring for her aged *grossmuder* made the winter days long in the cabin, and though there were her *mamm* and *daed* also, Martha was the most able-bodied and handy.

And then there was the problem of Judah . . .

Tall, pompous Judah Umble had been pursuing her since she'd turned sixteen, but there was something about him that made her cold at times . . . Not the clean cold of a winter's *nacht*, like now, she thought . . . but rather a cold of the soul that she could not quite explain. She pushed away thoughts of Judah, not wanting to interrupt her mental peace, and finally reached the creek. Casting a quick, perceptive glance around, she dropped the axe and her armload of things and began to strip down to her bare skin.

The cold exhilarated, and she gave a little squeal of delight as she ran and plunged, toes first, into the swirling water. She stood for a moment, her unbound hair caught in the current, and gloried in simply being alive . . .

Despite the hard work he did on a daily basis, it was not an unusual occurrence that twenty-year-old Joel Umble couldn't sleep. The hour was nigh on ten o'clock, he knew, but the moonlight that slid through the single window of his and Judah's room beckoned him somehow. He knew his *bruder* would scorn him for such ideas as the call of the moon, but for once, he didn't seem to care. He slid naked from his narrow bed and went to the window, the sill just bumping his lean hip. He pressed his forehead against the cold glass and felt his restlessness grow, especially when Judah began to snore.

A brisk walk in the snow, he thought, turning to quickly get into his clothes with as little noise as possible. He'd become adept over the years at slipping out of the *haus*, seeking peace and time alone, away from Judah's cruelty and his *mamm*'s anxious thoughts. And tonight was no exception. He crossed the kitchen, stopped to stroke his mother's cat, Puddles, and then went out into the *nacht*.

It was times like this that he missed his *fater* most of all—the great, tall man who'd slung him over a broad shoulder and galloped along like the fastest horse—they'd often shared a walk in the woods together. His *daed* had taught him the ways of nature and the wild, letting Joel see the Living *Gott* in every tree, leaf, and creature. It had been a blessing to have such a man in his life, even if it had only been for a short time.

He walked easily now through the deep snow, hands fisted and stuffed in the pockets of his heavy black coat. He pulled his dark hat down closer as the wind picked up, then nearly stopped still when the sound of a woman's voice came to him, high, melodic, carried by the *nacht* air from the nearby creek like a siren's song.

He followed the sound, finding himself strangely drawn toward it, then came to an abrupt stop at the edge of the creek bank when he saw the naked back of a girl. He retreated partially behind a nearby pine tree, but she soon stopped singing, as if aware somehow of his presence.

She turned in the water and he stared, transfixed

11

from his half-hidden position—at twenty years old, he'd never seen a woman's body before.

"Who's there?"

He caught his breath when he recognized Martha Yoder . . . He realized that he'd been too busy looking at her body to notice her face, but now he turned and pressed his back hard against the tree.

"No one," he muttered, answering her before he could help himself.

"I'm getting out. Don't tell me it's not you, Judah Umble! How dare you spy on me like this . . ."

*Judah? Ach, praise* Gott *she thinks it's my bruder* . . . Though the image of her white skin was burned into his brain. He felt hesitantly for the ground beneath his boots and had started to move away when he tripped and sprawled face forward in the snow . . .

Martha was furious. Not only did the man have the nerve to seek her out in broad daylight, now he was stalking her by the light of the moon. She grabbed up her pile of clothing and hastily put it on, careless of the pin fastenings that pricked her skin here and there, and marched over to where he was moving, scrambling to get to his feet.

"*Gut* for you—falling on your face, Judah," she pronounced to the tall frame of the man. His hat had come off, and his black hair seemed more tousled than usual in the half light. She hugged her belongings to her and waited for him to rise. He seemed to be taking a long time about it . . . "Are you hurt?" she finally snapped in exasperation.

"*Nee*," he whispered. "Just *geh*."

She tossed her head. "Judah Umble, I can't leave you lying here in the snow. You'll freeze to death."

"And you won't?"

"*Nee*, I won't. I've got the blood for it. Now, get up."

She sighed and reached a single arm down to tug fretfully at his coat sleeve, and then lost her balance, her toes colder than she cared to admit. She gave a small cry as she pitched forward on her hands and knees in the snow, and she saw his head turn out of the corner of her eye.

Then she gasped, amazed and shamed. Her bottom lip began to quiver. "Joel?"

# Chapter Two

Martha stared into his dark blue eyes, knowing the color by heart, even in the play of shadows and moonlight. Joel Umble was all she ever dreamed of, but he was as far away as a star—much too intelligent for her, and twice as beautiful, in her mind.

The hot, heavy fall of the inside of his wool coat hit her back, shaking her from her reverie. "What—?" she gasped, breaking off in a squeak as he swung her up into his arms, nestling her against the breadth of his chest.

"I'll have you home as quickly as I can," he said, his husky voice soothing. "Relax against me. It's all right."

Martha brushed away the hot tears that threatened to freeze on her cheeks. It was one thing to know that he was speaking to her as he might a hurt child or an injured creature, but quite another to think that he'd seen her nakedness. If Judah had seen her, it wouldn't have mattered so much—his eyes stripped her bare every time he looked at her. But Joel . . . *Joel is so* gut *and kind and pure . . .*

"It's not all right," she struggled to say as more tears tightened her throat. "You—you saw me."

"It was dark. Calm down."

He maneuvered her in his strong arms until she had no choice but to lean her head against his chest. She heard the thud of his heart and smelled the rich male scent of his throat where his shirt gave way a bit. She was as close to him as she could ever hope to be, and she was utterly miserable.

After a few moments of feeling the rhythm of his long strides, though, she began to surrender to the warmth of his coat all around her. He'd even settled his strong, dimpled chin on top of her head, surrounding her with more heat. She began to feel a permeating lassitude and closed her eyes, as if in a dream.

"No sleeping," he said in clear instruction as he dipped his head near her ear.

"I'm—not," she protested, slurring her words with a secret smile; she fancied that she sounded like creek water moving over smooth stones.

"Martha . . ."

"Hmmm?"

She tilted her head back against his shoulder and lifted her chin to the moonlight. *Joel Umble is carrying me home . . .* She felt him sigh, a heavy exhalation and play of his chest: first out, then in. She tried to lift her lashes with lazy intent, to look up at him, but she couldn't quite garner the energy. She half smiled at the effort and arched her back. She thought she heard what sounded like a groan reverberate through him, and then she was blinkingly, fiercely awake as his mouth came down on hers in a firm caress. She'd never been kissed before and had no idea how to respond, but the intimate touch was over so quickly that she thought maybe she'd imagined it.

She stared up at the firm line of his jaw. "Did—did you kiss me?"

She felt him shrug, then nestle her closer.

"I've never kissed before," he confessed.

*Joel Umble has never kissed before, when he has a mouth that seems made for such things . . .* She couldn't believe it.

He went on a few more steps, then cleared his throat. "Was it—right?"

"I've never kissed before either," she whispered.

She watched him swallow hard and then he nodded. "We're here."

Joel knew, without a shadow of a doubt, that if Bishop Loftus had found out about his and Martha's . . . meeting, he'd be seeking his wedding bed that *nacht* instead of his own narrow mattress. Fortunately (especially for Martha's sake), he'd been able to make it back to his room without notice. He undressed and slipped into bed, then turned to face the wall. Tentatively, he touched his lips in the darkness, still feeling the tingle from Martha's sweet mouth. He furrowed his brow in confusion.

*What was this thing called kissing? How did it* kumme *about? What was Adam's first kiss to Eve like? Probably better than I managed . . .*

As he recalled the honeyed sweetness of Martha's mouth, he ran a hand down his body beneath the warmth of the quilt and found himself aroused. He closed his eyes against the sensation and rolled over, trying not to think of Martha Yoder. But the images that appeared with luminous intensity in his mind would not be denied—hair like summer wheat shimmering in the moonlight; wide, questing brown eyes; full, pouty lips that seemed to beg to be touched with his tongue . . . His mouth watered, and he shifted restlessly.

He understood enough about desire to know it to be *Gott*-given, not some strange sin like Judah purported it to be. But he also knew that he'd seen Martha Yoder that *nacht* as only a husband should—*if a husband ever would take the time to discover a wife in such a wondering way . . .* From what he'd gathered with talk among the married men his age, bedding a wife seemed more like a grope and a gamble, all fervor and no finesse. Not that he understood any better, of course . . .

Yet after what had happened tonight—seeing

17

her naked body, then kissing her with a quick passion he didn't know he possessed, he realized there was only one thing to do. The honorable thing. He had to ask Martha to court with him. The thought brought a smile to his lips and increased his arousal.

Not that she'd seemed to expect any such action as courting on his part. He smothered a moan, pressing harder into the mattress, when he remembered setting her down on the porch of her family's cabin. She'd stepped from his arms and coat, when he would have gladly let her take it, but then she'd stood almost proudly in the chill wind, her spine straight and her shoulders back. "Thank you for carrying me home, Joel Umble." She'd lifted her chin and tossed her head like a wild filly, and he'd felt a rush of respect and awe for the girl as he'd helplessly traced the curved lines of her body beneath her clothing . . . Then she'd slipped inside and was gone.

He'd stood holding his coat in the chill, moonlight air, bereft but for the deep desire stirring within him. He'd shrugged into the heavy black wool, still warm from her body, and he'd started for home.

Now he drew in a deep breath and forced himself to close his eyes, only to jump when Judah kicked the side of his bed and he woke to realize that it was gray dawn.

"Well, why are ya up so early, girlie?" Martha's *grossmuder*, Esther Yoder, propped herself up on a stick-thin elbow on her bed near the woodstove and muttered the question in her ninety-year-old voice.

*Because Joel Umble carried me home last* nacht *and I haven't been able to think about anything else but him, and his scent, and his mouth, and . . .*

"I couldn't sleep much," she murmured, grabbing the egg basket in preparation to go out to the small barn before starting breakfast.

"Here now, at least put on yer wrap. Ye'll freeze." Her grandmother's order was tempered by fondness, and Martha dragged the dark blue shawl off the peg by the door with reluctance. There were so many mended holes in the garment that it provided little warmth, but she loved her grandmother and knew the *auld* woman's eyesight could not discern the relative uselessness of the fabric.

"I'll be right back," Martha said softly, not wanting to wake her aged and ill parents in the other room.

She stepped out onto the snow-dusted porch and ruthlessly thrust aside the image of Joel's handsome face as she marched down the two rickety steps. "He's not for the likes of you, my girl," she muttered aloud, admonishing herself.

*Nee, Joel Umble deserves someone like the local healer, May Miller, perhaps. May is a match for him, if not in beauty, then certainly in brains, while I am simply a dumm—*

"Hello, Martha."

She jumped as Judah Umble stepped out from behind the barn door right as she opened it.

"Judah! You scared me to death. I told you not to *kumme* around here anymore." She moved to brush past him, but he caught her arm in a tight grasp.

She looked up into his narrow brown eyes, which contained not a fraction of the warmth she saw in the magnetic blue of his *bruder*'s. She felt a flash of uncertainty. For the first time, she regretted letting Joel carry her home, even though it had brought a moment of excitement to her otherwise dreary life. Had she made a terrible mistake? *Is it possible that Joel told Judah about the previous* nacht *and now Judah thinks he might further push his intentions toward me?*

"Let me go," she demanded, trying to wrench her arm away, but he held her fast, and she knew she'd later find bruises on her skin.

"*Nee*, my dear." He shook her a bit, and she had the urge to knock him over the head with the egg basket, but she held back, wanting to see if her reputation on the mountain, what little of it there was, would be permanently ruined.

"What do you want?" she asked finally.

"I dreamed of you last *nacht*, as if you didn't already know," he sneered.

"What do you mean?"

"I know you work spells somehow by bathing in the rushing creek. You have *nee* shame, Martha Yoder. For anyone can see your nakedness."

Martha felt her heart sink. *So Joel did tell his* bruder . . . *The handsome man isn't what I thought he was . . .*

Judah shook her again, and this time her teeth rattled. "I saw your nakedness just a week ago. You were singing to the spirits as the water brewed around your nude body."

The nonsense about her singing to the spirits went over her head as she realized Judah had seen her—and he hadn't mentioned the previous *nacht*. "You saw me bathing—last week?" she whispered.

"That's what I said, Martha," he growled.

She was used to his inappropriate glances, but now her hands instinctively tried to cover her body with the basket, even though she was fully clothed.

He gritted his teeth. "You've hexed me, girl. You continue to entice me to the creek to burn yourself into my mind. And I've known you long enough now to understand that you won't lift the curse, will you?" For a brief moment a plea echoed in his tone.

"You're *narrish*," she said evenly.

21

She was unprepared for the slap he sent cracking across her cheek. She would have fallen if he hadn't held her upright. Her eyes welled with tears against her will. She wanted to scream for help, but her frail family was no match for Judah's strength.

"If you think I'm a hex, you'd better let me go," she warned.

But clearly his superstitions didn't extend to the rational, and he merely laughed out loud. He leaned down into her face and bit out each word. "One day, I will enjoy beating the evil from your snow-white skin."

This time she did swing the egg basket, but he merely slapped her again, almost as if doing a necessary duty. She tasted blood and saw the strange heat in his gaze as he licked his bottom lip. *Why, the man is aroused by striking me!* Her stomach turned and she tried, horrified, to step away, but his grip tightened.

"Listen very carefully, Martha, for *Derr Herr* has spoken to the *gut* Bishop Loftus, and he has instructed me as to what to do to save your soul. I will court you for an appropriate amount of time, and then I will marry you. I will keep your belly filled with child and your mouth bound shut until you can do no more harm to me or any other man. And if you refuse me in marriage, I am prepared to do as *Gott* would demand and expose you before all the community for your wicked ways.

Then both you and your family will be shunned."

For the first time his gaze softened. Not much, but enough to keep her wondering just what his intentions were. He brushed his hand over her cheek in an almost tender gesture. *He truly is* narrish. "But I would rather see you saved, Martha," he said in a low voice. "And you know your poverty-stricken family needs the support of the community. Do you understand what I say?"

Martha wanted to dispute his claim, to tell him what she thought about his hellfire, but the truth in his words and the unfamiliar madness in his eyes kept her mute, so she could only nod in agreement.

"*Gut*," he whispered, finally releasing her so abruptly that she fell to her knees before him. He stared down at her with dispassion again. "Very *gut*."

He left the barn, and Martha expelled the breath she found she'd been holding. *I'll tell someone,* her mind screamed, and then she lowered her head in despair, for she could not bear the thought of shaming her family so with her own behavior. She knew Judah took his spiritual instruction from the dark Bishop Loftus, never stopping to think on his own. The bishop would surely support his claim. She had no other strong kin to turn to, and she believed every word Judah had said about exposing her. For the briefest of moments, she once more felt Joel's strong arms around her, comforting and secure, but she could never bring the ugliness of Judah's threat out into the open when it might turn *bruder* against *bruder*. She let her bruised face fall into her hands for a moment, then cried out to *Gott*.

"Help me, *Derr Herr*. *Sei se gut*, help me!"

# Chapter Three

"You know your *bruder*'s crazy, don't you?"

Joel rolled his eyes at his best friend, Stephen Lambert, as they worked in the snug barn, pitching hay from the vast mows down to the stock below. Stephen was a hired hand around the farm who helped out wherever he was needed.

"He's not crazy," Joel said. "He's—religiously fervent." *And crazy . . . and torturous . . . and cruel—and the* bruder *I am called to love . . .*

"Uh-huh. I met him walking through the woods on my way over here this morning, and the man was muttering something about women and curses—not that women can't be a curse."

Joel grinned. "You tell that to Rose Raber, why don't you?"

Stephen had the grace to flush, but then pointed the pitchfork handle briefly in Joel's direction. "*Jah*, and you tell it to her sister, Ruby."

"There's nothing to tell," Joel said as his mind flew back to the moment he'd first seen Martha in the creek. Somehow now, Ruby Raber's renowned beauty and charm could do nothing to equal the vision he'd held in his arms the previous *nacht*. *And the woman I plan on courting—if she'll have me.*

Stephen's snort brought him back to the

moment. "See, you're daydreaming about her already, Joel. Better get to courting, I say."

"Perhaps I'll take your advice and—" He was cut off by a woman's shrill scream. Mamm! "*Ach, nee* . . ." He dropped the pitchfork and hurried down the ladder to the barn floor.

"Do you need help?" Stephen called from above.

"*Danki*. But if Judah's not around, Mamm'll do better with me alone." Joel trudged as fast as he could through the thick snow to the cabin, having no idea what he'd find and praying his words to Stephen were true. His mother favored Judah, and her preferential treatment to her older son had always confused Joel.

His *mamm* was what folks on the mountain politely called "odd in the head"—not *narrish*, just odd. Joel knew the truth to be more that his mother had always been rather childlike. Upon his *fater*'s death, she had retreated further into a state of fearful anxiety that made her difficult to reach at times.

He pushed open the heavy back door of the *haus* and froze when his gaze landed on the bloody paw prints on the floor.

"*Ach*, Joel, where's Judah?" his *mamm* sobbed.

He went to her, standing a few steps away, and forced himself to remain calm. "Mamm," he said, measuring his tone and words, "tell me what happened."

26

Mamm's tears flowed down her thin cheeks. "I broke a glass and Puddles stepped on a sliver. I'm afraid it's still in his paw. I hurt him—oh, I hurt him!"

Joel took a quick glance at the big gray cat licking its front paw, looking more annoyed than hurt. He took another step toward his mother.

"Don't touch me." She recoiled.

"I know," he said soothingly. "I won't."

His mother didn't like him to touch her, especially when she was upset. But Joel had become expert at de-escalating situations like this over the years, even when he couldn't offer anything but the anchor of his voice. He often wondered what his *mamm* had been like when she was young and perhaps more carefree. Certainly her fears had grown since he was five, the time his *daed* had died from pneumonia.

"I'll have a look at the paw, all right?" he said.

His mother turned and gripped the bone-white sink with even whiter fingertips. "I can't watch," she wailed over her shoulder, rocking from front to back. "You know I can't watch!"

"No watching. It's fine." He bent and lifted Puddles into his arms. He felt the pad of the furry paw with tender fingers. Joel closed his eyes for a moment, visualizing the flesh. There was indeed a deep gash in the main pad and a protruding sliver of glass. "You're a tough old cat," he murmured. But as if to contradict Joel's words,

Puddles started to squirm when Joel skimmed the pointed edge of the glass. Better to yank out the sliver than to try to ease it out slowly; he extracted the glass with a quick movement that had Puddles clawing in his arms. Then, when Joel touched the injured paw once more, the cat quieted and finally stilled.

"Is it over?" Mamm asked, turning weakly from the sink.

"*Jah*. He is well."

"*Ach, gut*." She leaned against the sink, as if the Puddles ordeal had sapped all of her energy. "I was so worried."

"There's *nix* to worry about." Joel held out the cat to his mother. "See? He's fine."

"Then I didn't do anything wrong?"

"*Nee*. Everything is all right."

She sighed, her eyes red from crying. "Thank *Derr Herr*. I was so worried and—" She broke off, and Joel frowned as the door banged open and Judah entered, stamping his boots on the braided rug.

"What's this mess?" Judah asked, gesturing to the floor.

"Puddles cut his foot." Mamm's voice trembled. "*Ach*, Judah—I wish you'd been here."

"It's all right, Mamm," Judah said softly.

Joel watched him gather their mother in his arms, and once more, he was struck by the almost odd sway his *bruder* seemed to hold over their parent. *But families stick together on Ice Mountain, no matter how odd . . .*

Then Judah stepped through the bloody paw prints and put a hand out to stroke the back of the cat where it nestled in Joel's arms. "*Ach, jah—*the pretty cat." Judah's movements were gentle, but his tone was not.

Puddles squalled and jumped down, skidding out of the room as if his tail had been scalded.

Judah's lips curved into a sharp grin. "A pity the glass didn't run deeper." He looked directly at Joel. "It will give me great pleasure to skin that cat one day."

"Judah," Joel warned in a low tone. "You'll upset Mamm."

But his *bruder* merely laughed and reached out a hand to pat their *mamm*'s shoulder. "She knows I only jest. What good would a cat pelt be, hmmm?" Then Joel watched him leave the room.

Joel glanced at the smeared trail of blood on the floor, then at his mother, who was not shaking now. "He was only joking, Mamm. He didn't mean it."

She shook her head, her eyes distant, looking at some past or future thing, but there was no condemnation in her words. "*Jah*, he does, Joel. Perhaps he does."

Joel drew a deep, steadying breath, pushing aside his mother's words, then grabbed a damp rag from the sink and began to clean the bloody floor.

Martha somehow managed to hide her tears and scramble the eggs she'd gathered, rationing out the bacon that had been a gift of May Miller by crumbling its fragrant crispiness into the eggs. May's gift had been much appreciated, but Martha had struggled with her pride when she'd received it. Everyone on Ice Mountain knew that Martha's family was poor—indeed, the poorest family in the Amish community. But Bishop Loftus encouraged folks not to "overdo" their support of the struggling Yoder family. The *gut* bishop had his own ideas about the poor, which didn't much coincide with the Bible's, Martha thought wearily. When she made up the trays for her parents and grandmother, there was little left over for her, but she gave up most of her portion gladly, knowing that the others needed the nourishment more.

"Martha, what have you eaten this morning, child?" her mother, Elise, asked with a wheeze from where she lay, propped up on a small pile of threadbare quilts.

Martha smiled cheerfully. "More than enough, Mamm." She put the tray on her mother's frail lap. "Your breathing sounds tight. I'll make a batch of May's tea for you right after you've eaten."

Her *mamm*'s asthma, always worse in the fall and winter, had been particularly bad lately, even though it was nearly spring. Martha suppressed a sigh of worry and turned to wake her *fater*, who slept in a bed positioned opposite his wife's. Chet Yoder had once been a stalwart vision of a man— tall, strong, and more than able to provide for his family. But a logging accident had rendered his body useless from the waist down, and his once-proud frame was now all but a hollow shell. Still worse, he was broken in spirit, Martha thought as she turned to tend her *daed*. He no longer seemed to seek after *Derr Herr* and frequently stared off into the distance as if attempting to capture the past and its happenings.

"How are you this morn, Fater?" Martha asked, not truly expecting a reply.

"Your mouth's bleedin', *Dochder*," Chet muttered, and she ducked her head away in surprise. "Don't chew your lips in the cold, Martha. It only brings ice and blood . . . ice and the taste of blood."

# Chapter Four

After the incident with his mother's cat, Joel continued the day's work as he absently twisted his red oak shepherd's crook and tried to concentrate on the book he held in one hand—an account of using selenium in pregnant ewes as a nutrient to improve fetal hardiness—but all of the writer's successful results vied with the vivid flesh and blood image of Martha Yoder. He glanced at the pale blue late-winter sky and chafed at the hours until dark when he could go and discover whether or not she would consider courting with him.

He was jolted back to awareness of the moment when one of his Clun Forest sheep nearly knocked him off balance with some good-natured attention-seeking. He looked down into the intelligent black face of the creature and recognized Lost Lenore, a ewe that had terrific maternal instincts, as long as she wasn't wandering off by herself into the forest to graze.

He glanced out over the peaceful flock of sheep, knowing each one of the seemingly confusing mass, by looks if not by name and personality. He ran a partial confinement operation, letting the flock forage beneath the snow for a few hours each day or else providing them with hay and then herding them indoors to be kept safe against the cold and the *nacht*.

His stomach rumbled and he knew it must be nearing dinnertime. His *mamm* was a *gut* cook, despite her anxieties, and he hoped she might serve apples and onions—a traditional favorite. He had started to herd the flock into their large barn when he heard a high feminine voice call his name.

"Joel Umble, what are you reading now?"

He looked up with a faint smile when he saw Stephen's love interest, Rose Raber, delicately picking her way across to the fence nearest him.

"Just a book. Stephen's up in the haymows."

He watched her narrow lips turn down briefly as she sniffed and gave a pat to her bonnet. "I was actually looking for you."

"Me?" He was surprised, and his quick mind figured that she was probably up to some scheme or another and wanted his help. *Poor Stephen . . . He doesn't stand a chance against a calculating female . . .* He came back to the moment to find Rose tapping an impatient shoe on a rock and thought helplessly of Martha's slender, pink feet in the snow the *nacht* before.

"Joel Umble—are you even listening to a word I've said?"

He smiled good-naturedly. "*Nee*, forgive me."

Her blue eyes sparkled for a moment, making him think of cold gems. "Certainly you're forgiven . . . I only came over to invite you, and your family, of course, to supper tomorrow *nacht*. You know we're to host the hymn sing, and Mamm thought it would be nice to have some guests beforehand."

"*Ach*, surely. I'll tell Mamm . . . and Judah, of course."

"I already saw Judah," she replied airily. "I stopped by Bishop Loftus's *haus* before I came here, and Judah was there."

*As always,* Joel thought tiredly. His *bruder* and the bishop seemed to be close, though Joel often found himself questioning the teachings of the community's spiritual leader. Then he thought of something.

"Uh—Rose—perhaps you might invite Martha Yoder to come as well?"

He cocked his head in confusion when the pleasant expression melted from the girl's face.

"Martha Yoder? Why Joel, she comes to church with patches on her dress . . . And besides, Bishop Loftus says that the Yoders . . . well, poverty, is a result of the hidden sin in their lives. I couldn't possibly have Martha Yoder there with Bishop Loftus sharing the same table."

"Why not?" Joel persisted, feeling angry at Rose's disdainful dismissal of Martha.

Rose gave a helpless shrug, and Joel clenched his shepherd's staff tighter. "Didn't *Derr Herr* Himself eat with the poor? And what sin do the

Yoders hide that *Gott* would so afflict them?"

Rose gave a quick, furtive look over one shoulder, then spoke low. "Joel, you musn't speak that way. You know that Bishop Loftus is a great spiritual leader, and to contradict him is . . ."

"Heresy?" Joel asked.

"What?"

"Never mind. We'll be at supper. *Sei se gut,* give our thanks to your *mamm* for the invitation."

Rose nodded and then hurried away, floundering for a moment with her skirts in the snow. He watched her go, unable to resist comparing Martha's natural grace to that of the other girl. Then he turned back to rub Lenore's black ears while he thought over his angry feelings about Bishop Loftus. The man gave him a sick feeling at times when he spoke of some parable or teaching in church, yet Joel had never really expressed his misgivings aloud—until now. He realized that perhaps it was no chance meeting that he'd had with Martha but rather something that would bring about change in his life and possibly others'. Then he gently prodded Lenore away and began to herd the sheep to shelter.

Martha's fragile jaw ached from the blows Judah had given her, and she swallowed hard as she stirred the outside kettle full of ashes and fat. She had to make soap whether she had been beaten or not, so she straightened her spine and began to hum as she worked. She tried not to think of the possibility that Judah might *kumme*, even that very *nacht*, to court her and shuddered to think of what that might entail. *But surely he would do no improper thing—not that slapping me was proper* . . . Still, she knew that bundling, or bed courtship, was a common practice among her people, and she could not stand the thought of lying so close to Judah, even with a bundling board between them.

Her thoughts drifted as she moved the paddle stick in the boiling mass, and then her attention was caught by the muted sound of her mother coughing hard inside the cabin. Martha abandoned the soap, careless of the mess she'd have to clean up later, and flew to the porch and then inside. She entered her parents' room to find her *mamm* caught in a deep paroxysm of coughing.

"*Ach*, Mamm," Martha strove to keep her voice calm. "I'll get some more of May Miller's tea for you right away."

"*Nee, Dochder*." Her *fater*'s worried voice gave her pause. "Yer *mamm*'s worse off this time. Best if you run over to May's and ask for some stronger kind of medicine. Take the brown hen with ya to barter."

"*Jah*." Martha nodded in hasty agreement, not bothering to contradict her *daed*. She knew that he understood from her own vivid descriptions of the chickens that the brown hen was their best layer—but the healer must be paid. *Even though she'll probably refuse it . . .*

Martha called reassurances to her *grossmuder*, then raced out to the shabby barn with the alarming sound of her *mamm*'s asthma echoing in her mind. She snatched up the surprised brown hen and tucked the bird under her arm and beneath her frayed cloak. Then she set off in desperate haste for May's cabin on its rocky incline.

Joel leaned back in the comfortable ladderback chair and took a drink of the black tea that May was in the habit of brewing when he came for an occasional visit. They both understood that there was nothing romantic in these brief encounters, but rather simply a shared love of reading and the written word.

"You're distracted," May murmured, and he smiled at her.

May was young, but her eyes held old secrets, and he always had the odd feeling around her that she could see more of him than he might prefer. But now, he wanted to talk about Martha . . .

"I guess I am a bit," he admitted, glancing to the small cabin's kitchen window at the falling dusk outside.

Courting was done mostly at *nacht* in the beginning, and he was counting the minutes until he could *geh* to Martha's.

"Who is she?" May asked, idly turning the pages of a poetry book she'd been reading aloud.

Joel laughed and shook his head. "Is it that obvious?"

"*Jah*," she answered simply.

He knew he could trust May's discretion, so he spoke Martha's name like a deep caress.

May nodded, smiling a bit. "An excellent match that would be—you and she."

"You say 'would be' . . . Do you think she won't have me?" He tried to keep the anxiousness from his voice and was surprised to find his heart pounding.

"I think—" May paused. "That love is never easy. Courting should be a time to truly get to know another person so that later . . . well, never mind."

"What?" He was intrigued but also deeply shaken by May's seemingly casual use of the word "love." *Do I love Martha Yoder? I don't even know her . . . but I want to.* Gott*, I want to . . .*

He was about to mutter this thought aloud when there was a furious pounding at the door. "Somebody's bad off," May murmured, and he rose to hurry and open the wood barrier.

Martha Yoder nearly fell into his arms, and he had difficulty keeping his hands to himself as he hastened to help her balance. She was gasping for breath, and her doe-brown eyes were wild with fright.

"Martha," he said soothingly. "What is it?" He took the hen from her without question and set it on the floor.

"My *mamm*," she cried. "She's coughing real bad—I don't think she can breathe much."

Joel saw that May was already working at the large cabinet that housed the mysteries of herbs and potions the woman used to bring health and healing to their people.

He caught Martha's small hand in his and automatically began to rub his thumb over the rapid pulse point in her wrist. He longed to gather her to him but he knew he might help a better way when May turned to both of them. She held a small vial of some reddish liquid.

"Here. Give her a few drops of this in water. It will both ease the coughing and calm her."

Joel gently released Martha's hand, not sure if she had even noticed his touch. He took the vial from May, then turned to look deep into Martha's eyes. "Let me run on ahead with the medicine to give your *mamm*. You're exhausted, and my legs are longer. Trust me. Please."

He saw the wavering indecision in her pale face, but then she nodded. "*Jah, sei se gut, geh. Danki.*"

Joel exhaled and nodded, then ran from the cabin, praying that *Gott* would get him there in time to help.

# Chapter Five

Martha drew several deep breaths as her eyes randomly swept the book-laden table at May Miller's. But worry for her mother held back any assumptions about Joel and May and she pulled her cloak closer, preparing to run after him.

"Wait, Martha, *sei se gut*," May called.

"*Ach*, do you have something else for Mamm? I hope the hen here will be enough in payment." Martha struggled to keep the anxiety out of her voice, knowing that surely, sooner or later, the healer would need payment that her family did not have to give.

May scooped the hen off the floor. "I'll not take your best layer, Martha."

"Wh—what? How did you know?"

Martha watched the other girl shrug. "I just know—the same way I also know that I've never seen Joel Umble so concerned about a woman as to hold her hand in comfort."

Martha felt herself flush. "Did he hold my hand?—I didn't notice."

May gave her back the hen, and Martha automatically settled the bird beneath her arm.

"Next time—notice," May suggested dryly. "Now, *geh* to your *mamm*."

Martha nodded. "*Danki.*" Then she turned and tried, in her too-tight shoes, to race home over the snowy ground.

Joel had never encountered poverty up close, so his first glimpse of the interior of Martha's home came as something of a shock. But he knew, in his heart, that it didn't matter where a person lived but rather how a person lived their life and loved. And clearly, Martha's home was one of love.

Her grandmother, whom he had only seen a few times over the years, smiled at him with bootblack eyes as she raised herself up on one elbow when he knocked at the cabin's door then entered without much preamble. "I've *kumme* with medicine for Martha's *mamm*," he said to the *auld* woman.

"In the room yonder, young fella. Where is my girlie, Martha?"

He crossed the sagging floor and smiled down at her. "She *kummes* behind me. Don't worry."

"How can I worry when there's a strapping lad like you ta help?" Frau Yoder demanded, and he nodded as he headed for the adjacent room. As he saw the invalids' beds, he wondered briefly where Martha slept, then gave his full attention to her *mamm*.

Elise Yoder still showed hints of a faded beauty, even as she clearly struggled to breathe.

"I need a cup to mix up the medicine that will ease you. It's from May Miller."

"Our family cup is out at the well," Martha's *fater* said over his wife's wheezing. "Ya passed it on the way in."

"Right." Joel nodded as he headed back outdoors, unable to resist thinking of the myriad cups and mugs his *mamm* had at home.

He grabbed the tin dipper, pulled up the well bucket and scooped water into the cup. He dropped a bit of the medicine into the cold water, then hurried back into the cabin, all the while thinking of how easy it would be for the community to gather and help the Yoders—but then there was Bishop Loftus to contend with . . . He pushed the rapid thoughts away as he helped Martha's *mamm* into an upright position and placed the cup to her lips. She drank, still fitfully coughing. As he pressed his hand against her back, he closed his eyes and pictured her damaged lungs working easily with the miracle of breath that only *Gott* can give—the breath of life.

He opened his eyes to an odd silence and glanced down into Frau Yoder's face, now peaceful and relaxed, her breathing even and easy.

"*Danki*, Joel Umble," she whispered.

He nodded, glad that the potion May had made worked so well, then unbent his back to stand upright as he realized that Martha stood behind him.

"What did you do?"

Joel turned to look at her, taken once more by the wild loveliness of her face and the toss of her honeyed hair, which had lost all of its pins as well as her *kapp*. He knew of no other *maedel* who would appear without the proper head covering in front of someone not her husband, but Martha was like no other girl.

"What did you do?" she demanded again, breaking his reverie.

He spread his hands helplessly. "I—I gave your *mamm* May's medicine. What else could I do?"

She looked straight at him, deep into his eyes, then finally dropped her gaze. "I think you might be able to do a whole lot, Joel Umble. A whole lot . . ."

Martha was quiet as she saw him to the broken front steps of the little cabin. She thought he would take his leave quickly—probably anxious to get back to May as the *nacht* settled in . . .

"Where do you sleep?" he asked.

His soft, intimate question amazed her, and she answered automatically. "In the pantry." She gestured with her hand to the narrow add-on to the left side of the cabin. "It has a window," she added, not wanting to arouse his pity.

"*Gut*," he said, smiling in a way that made her

43

feel like she stood on uneven ground, lost in the blue of his eyes.

"Why?" she finally managed to ask. "Why is it good?"

She watched the rise and fall of his broad chest as he drew a deep breath. He leaned close to her, bending his head so that his dark hair brushed her heated cheek. "Because I want to court you, Martha Yoder. I want to throw pebbles at your window and beg to *kumme* in, and you might let me and we'll—"

"Because you saw my body—you want to court me?" She knew she sounded curious, not angry. *Joel Umble is asking to court me . . .* Ach*, Gott, help me. Help me know what to do . . .*

She shivered when he finally whispered against her cheek, his thick lashes lowered. "*Jah*," he whispered. "Because I saw you—it is only honorable that I ask to court you. Please, Martha—let me."

He reached his long fingers to caress her jaw, and she nearly winced. Then all thoughts of courting with Joel flew out of her mind as she remembered Judah.

She backed away from Joel's tall warmth and edged up the steps. "*Nee*, Joel. I—I cannot court with you because of desire. It—it isn't right." *But it is . . . It is . . . It feels so right, if not for Judah and his very real threats.* And then she realized that she was worried what evil Judah might do to

Joel if he found out his own *bruder* was courting the girl he'd set his sights on . . . She shuddered and made for the cabin door.

"Martha," he said in the growing dusk.

She couldn't help but turn at his even tone. "*Jah*?"

"I'm not giving up." He cleared his throat. "I'm going to keep asking, keep wanting, and I think—I hope—maybe you will too."

She shook her head and mutely entered her home, closing the door on him and the dream of any future she might fantasize about with Joel Umble.

# Chapter Six

"Quite a nice spread, wouldn't you say, Joel?" Bishop Loftus spoke loudly in a jovial tone that nonetheless had rivulets of darkness running through it.

Joel knew the *auld* man well enough to realize that any response could be twisted into a sermon on evil, so he merely nodded politely.

They were standing in the Rabers' well-appointed cabin for the Saturday *nacht* supper that Rose had invited him and his family to attend before the youth singing. The long kitchen table was covered in a snowy white cloth and was laden with so much food that it was a wonder the legs held. Any other time, Joel would have joined in the conversation and appreciated the bountiful dishes, but now, all he could see in his mind's eye was Martha's sparse cabin, and he wondered if the Yoder family had enough to eat that *nacht*.

Judah stood on the opposite side of the bishop while Frau Raber, Rose and Ruby's mother, busily moved about the room. Herr Raber began a rumbling conversation with Joel about wool that distracted him for the moment from his concerns about the Yoder family, and soon it was time to eat.

Joel slid onto the bench, finding Ruby pressed

near him as everyone strove to fit, and he wondered if the girl had purposely asked her *mamm* to add no extra chairs so that she might snuggle close. Though he might have enjoyed the feminine touch in the past, he now found it cloying and wondered how a simple few minutes with Martha in his arms could have changed him so much. *But it wasn't simple—it was hot and right and filled me with a desire beyond myself . . .*

He looked up from the silent grace late to realize that dishes were being passed around him. He concentrated on scooping out a spoonful of sweet potatoes covered in thick marshmallow, then handed the casserole to Ruby. She made a subtle play of pressing against his side, and he nearly rolled his eyes.

"Spring is nearly upon us," Bishop Loftus observed. "Only a few more days away. The time for courting, I always say."

Joel frowned faintly. Adults were never to intrude on the process of courting—another young person might know certain details, but initially, most courting was done in secret— which gave him an idea.

"Everything is delicious tonight, as always," Joel announced, distracting everyone's attention from the bishop's turn of conversation.

"*Danki*, Joel." Ruby smiled. "Mamm and Rose and I did our best."

He nodded and gestured lightly to the table.

"Such blessings of abundance, there are bound to be leftovers."

Frau Raber spoke up quickly. "*Jah*, Joel—and we would love for you and your family to take some home."

Joel drew a deep breath. "I was actually thinking of taking some up to the Yoder family. They've—been on my heart lately."

He was unprepared for the dagger-sharp glares he received from both the bishop and Judah, and he shrugged innocently. "After all, we are to help the poor as *Derr Herr* commands . . . Isn't that right, Bishop Loftus?"

Joel lifted his gaze to meet the dark eyes of the bishop directly. He knew he was treading a thin line, but he didn't care. If it was within his power, Martha and her family would taste sweet potatoes and marshmallow that *nacht* too.

Bishop Loftus took a long sip from his coffee mug, then nodded abruptly with an odd glance at Judah. "*Jah*, Joel Umble, you speak correctly. The poor should be helped, but not indulged. It's not *gut* for them and will only keep them bound in the curse of their poverty."

*Here we go* . . . Joel sat up straighter. He tapped his fork idly against the table and nodded. "The curse of poverty—I've heard you say that before, Bishop. So you believe that young Martha Yoder, caring alone for three invalids, is cursed? How so?"

The table had grown still and silent, and Joel waited, counting his heartbeats, but then the bishop laughed, breaking the tension. "*Ach*, Frau Umble, your *sohn* has wit as well as intelligence to try to ask such questions at a festive meal . . . We will eat and talk of other—more meaningful things this *nacht*."

And Joel listened as the people gathered strove to make relieved conversation, almost as if an icy knife had passed through their midst but had done no real harm. He went back to eating his meal but was aware of the bishop's eyes upon him, almost as if he were being weighed somehow. Rose shot him a daggered look across the table that warned him to forget the Yoders.

But he smiled at her, then turned to his other side, where his hostess sat. "Frau Raber, as I said, if you might pack up the leftovers—" he began in an undertone.

She passed him the scalloped potatoes and gave a brief nod. "At the back door, during the singing."

He recognized a kindred spirit and went on to finish the meal in better spirits. *At least not everyone blindly follows the commands of the bishop . . .*

Martha leaned over on her hands and knees, scrubbing the hardwood floor and trying to ignore the familiar light-headed sensation that always came at the end of a long day of work and little food. Her grandmother had accidentally spilled some water on the floor, and Martha had decided she might as well scrub the entire area under the *auld* woman's bed. She finished and blew out a breath to cool her forehead, sitting back on her heels.

"You had less than a spoonful of that oatmeal ya cooked for supper, dearie," Esther Yoder murmured, leaning over the side of her bed.

Martha smiled at her and reached out to pat her grandmother's blue-veined hands. "It doesn't matter. Tomorrow I will make an extra batch of scrambled eggs." Her belly growled at the thought, and she laughed.

A brisk knock on the door broke her good humor, and she got to her feet, worrying wearily that it might be Judah. But when she opened the door and stepped outside to keep the chill from her *grossmuder*, she saw nothing but a large wicker basket.

She picked it up tentatively, glancing around, then caught the rich scent of baked ham from within. She hastened indoors and set the basket on the floor.

"What is it, dearie?"

Martha lifted the latch and pulled up the lid. She felt dizzy for a moment at the sight of so much food crowding the wicker confines to bulging capacity.

"It's—food," Martha said slowly, trying to reason who might bring such bounty to their home. *Surely not Judah? If anything, he'd think starving was* gut *for us . . . But, perhaps, Joel? Nee, not when I shut him out so coldly . . .* She realized her grandmother was speaking and answered with haste.

"What? I'm sorry—I was only thinking of who might—"

"*Derr Herr,* that's Who," Esther said briskly. "Now, *kumme.* Serve it up, and make your own plate first, my girlie."

Martha obeyed, overwhelmed by such bounty. Baked ham and coleslaw; scalloped potatoes and mashed, sweet potatoes with marshmallow and rich brown gravy in a carefully placed cup. And coconut cream pie, as well as half an apple streusel. Why, such an amount could last them for days, Martha thought. *If I'm careful . . .*

She portioned out plates, adding just a spoonful more to everyone else's but her own. Then she sat down next to her grandmother in a rickety chair and ate slowly and with thankfulness. She had been worried what they would do with the pantry running so very low and the potatoes nearly gone, but soon it would be spring and she might plant the garden, which always sustained them for a good long while.

She balanced her plate on her knees and

savored the rich taste of marshmallow and sweet potatoes, wondering against her will what Joel Umble was doing that *nacht*.

Joel stood in the dark cold, back in the trees behind Martha's cabin. He shifted his weight from one leg to the other to keep warm and hoped that the Yoders would find the food sustaining. He was waiting until he saw a candle through the window of the small pantry, indicating that Martha was in her room, and then he would try to ask her once more whether she might court with him.

He rationalized as he waited, hoping she wouldn't think the food came from him. He had seen the proud lift of her chin and knew that she would not like to accept charity, especially if she might somehow associate it as a bribe to win her favor. He sighed aloud at the thought, then nearly jumped out of his skin when the play of a lantern shone through the trees. *Someone is coming along this way—and at such a late hour of* nacht.

He immediately stood taut, wondering if the person meant harm to the Yoders.

"Joel?"

He lifted his head at the harsh sound of his name and turned to face the tall man behind the lantern.

# Chapter Seven

Martha startled upright on her meager bed when a spatter of pebbles struck the glass window on the opposite wall just a few feet away. Dear *Gott*, it's Judah already . . . She flung back her thin quilt and sat upright, her breathing sounding harsh to her own ears. It was typical of her people to court initially in secret, at *nacht*, when the others of the girl's *haus* were asleep. But in her thin *nacht*gown, she felt almost defenseless, for she knew that nothing would change Judah's resolve. She swallowed, and her bare toes curled back from the icy wood floor as she went to the door of the shed that was her bedroom and opened the latch. For a moment, she saw nothing but dark, and then a tall figure stepped into the light of the guttering candle she had on the wooden box that was her makeshift nightstand.

She bit her lip and looked up into his face, then gasped in surprise as he easily removed his hat. "Joel?"

"*Jah*," he whispered. "May I—would you allow me to *kumme* in?"

"Wh—why?" she asked, not caring now

about the cold. Just having the chance to talk with him alone seemed warm and heartening somehow.

He cleared his throat. "I've told you. I want to court you, Martha."

She stared up into his blue eyes and felt a stunning lassitude begin to steal over her. Perhaps this would be a chance for a moment of happiness against what she knew would only be misery at Judah's hands. Maybe *Gott* had sent Joel to her . . .

She widened the door and he stepped in, ducking his head beneath the low wood frame. She waited while he shut out the cold, her hands fisted with desire at her sides, her longing to touch him so great she could taste it.

"Martha?"

He stepped so close to her she could smell the subdued pine of his soap, and she shivered. She arched her back and watched with some inborn womanly knowledge as his gaze lowered and his handsome face flushed.

He moved quickly, catching her hard against him until she could feel his own body's response, and then he was kissing her, slanting his head, using his tongue, until she closed her eyes in wanton desire and tangled her arms about his broad shoulders.

He bit her bottom lip cruelly and her eyes flew open . . . She tasted blood at the exact moment she recognized Judah's mocking face . . .

Joel stared at the man who held the lantern in the dark woods and had the curious sensation that he was falling, even though his legs held firm. He blinked, trying to see better, when he suddenly felt as though a chasm had opened somewhere in time, directly in front of him. He was powerless to turn from the vision, a hazy scene that brought the metallic taste of blood to his mouth and an incredible certainty that death loomed somewhere near. And then it was gone and he stood staring at his old friend, welcoming the sharp glare of the lantern light.

"*Buwe*, you look like you expect a ghost. Don't ya know your friend, Ole Dan Zook?"

Joel exhaled and half laughed, reaching to shake the other man's big hand. "Dan—*nee*, I didn't know you in the dark." He strove to keep his voice steady. "What are you doing out here at this time of *nacht*?"

Dan Zook lived up in the high timber and had been a friend to Joel's *daed*. Joel could remember sitting on the *auld* mountain man's knee when he was little more than a toddler. When Joel's *daed* had passed away, it had been Dan who had often filled in the gaps in Joel's knowledge of the woods and who'd continued to foster in him a love of its creatures.

"Well," Dan grunted, "I know what I'm doing about here—hanging some smoked fish in the Yoders' barn. But what about you?"

Joel shook his head in the light of the lifted lantern. "Something similar, I guess."

Dan threw back his great head and laughed. "I knowed you since you was little, Joel Umble. And you can't fool *auld* Dan. You're hanging around in the dark waitin' ta court that Yoder *maedel*, am I right?"

Joel had to smile. Normally, the absolute secrecy of courting was of the utmost importance, but he'd already told May, whom he knew he could trust, and he knew that admitting his intentions to Dan would feel good. Besides, Dan lived far from the reach of Bishop Loftus and any community gossip; he'd been shunned two years before because he'd dared to have words with the bishop during a preaching sermon. Joel didn't remember the text, but he had known Dan was right when he heard him speak. And Dan had been able to make it on his own, living off the land. Joel knew that he wasn't technically supposed to be speaking to a shunned Amish person, but he also knew he'd acknowledge Dan anywhere.

"*Jah*," Joel said softly, coming back to the moment. "I seek to court Martha Yoder, but she doesn't seem to want me."

Old Dan sighed. "The child's as wild as the wind; you won't be able to reach her with your words or books, I don't imagine."

*Books!* Joel thought quickly, ignoring his friend's advice. *I'll write her a poem or a letter . . . Words on a page are harder to deny at times than those spoken . . .* He was thankful to have something to concentrate on besides his eerie vision.

"*Ach, buwe* . . . I can fair hear the wheels turnin' in that head of yours. I should have kept me big mouth shut. Well, I'll be headin' on. Looks like there's a bit of candlelight in the small window yonder. *Gott*'s peace be with ya, *sohn*."

Joel embraced the *auld* mountain of a man in the dark after Dan had dimmed the lantern. "*Danki* . . . I'll *kumme* up and see you soon, my friend. And Dan . . . be careful, will you?"

Dan grunted, then stepped on, his large frame barely making a sound on the snowy ground.

Joel turned back to the Yoders' cabin and found that his heart was throbbing at his pulse points and he felt as though he'd run a long mile through sodden earth, but he ignored all of this as he headed for the small door of Martha's pantry bedroom.

• • •

Martha sat bolt upright in bed, stifling a scream after her heated dream had turned to a nightmare, but somehow she steeled her heart and set her jaw with determination . . . She knew then that if Joel Umble should ever *kumme* courting, she'd let him in and—*Well. I'll let him in, if only for a few moments. And I'll be able to live off of whatever he says or does even in a lifetime spent with Judah . . .*

Joel threw the pebble lightly, striking the glass in the window with accuracy. He held his breath as he considered the charged implications of his actions. The hard stone against the fragility of the glass, begging for entry—it was all too symbolic of what a man's body did with a woman's, and it left him feeling hot inside his wool coat, despite the cold of the air.

Then the candlelight wavered and the small door to the pantry room was opened a bit, cascading mellow warmth out into the snow. He half smiled, feeling oddly close to tears. He was in . . .

It was odd, but it seemed almost as though Martha had been waiting for him. She seemed very practical in her movements as she held the door wider for him to duck and enter. He slipped off his hat, then rose to his full height in the narrow room.

He glanced at the sparse space between her handmade willow bed and the shelf housing the limited preserves of the family. Two canned jars of venison, a few green beans, and a pint of crushed tomatoes. *Nothing on which to sustain a family for very long . . .*

"Did you *kumme* to take an accounting of our food supplies, Joel Umble?" she asked in brisk tones, and he swung his gaze back to her.

"*Nee*," he said huskily. "And what limit I might see on the shelves is more than made up for by the bounty you provide to the eye."

She tilted her head as if weighing the value of his words, and he was struck by the slender outline of her body in her thin cotton *nacht*gown. He wasn't completely sure, but he thought that most of the time, Amish girls courted with their hair up and their skirts down, but he was beginning to understand that Martha would do as she pleased—tradition or not.

She was standing with her hands folded in front of her, pressed against the back wall of the sliver of a room, and she looked like he felt: half scared, but wide-eyed with excitement. She was illuminated beauty in the midst of darkness . . . save for the single candle that guttered on a small table at the head of the bed.

"Do you want me here?" he asked finally. He wondered if she heard the note of hope that lingered in the air with his whispered question.

He watched her pale face, her eyes shining like pools of autumn sunshine, and could barely suppress his sigh of relief when she nodded.

"*Jah*," she whispered back, and then slowly moved her right hand to indicate the bed. "Would—do you want to sit?"

He moved to sit down gingerly on the edge of the bed with its tattered quilt cover, unsure if the wood would hold his weight—but it did, after an alarming creak or two. He drew a deep breath, trying to relax, when Martha stepped forward, only to sink down beside him. Her thigh pressed against his, and Joel felt the overwhelming sensation that his heart would pound out of his chest.

"You nervous?" she ventured, and he nodded, unable to stop himself.

"You shouldn't be," she went on, almost wistfully. "You got a nice *haus*, nice clothes, and such—money. I'm half ashamed to have you here in this shack. But it's mine and who I am."

Joel looked at her then. "I'd wager the dreams you dream in this little room are as great as those dreamed in palaces far away. I'm not a snob, Martha."

"*Nee*, I wasn't saying that. I just—" She paused, and he grasped the moment, leaning over to press his mouth to hers.

He drew away after a second, and she stared at him, then spoke. "I guess we should practice for longer, if we want to get *gut* at it." There was both anxiety and an odd note of sadness in her voice.

But he half smiled. "You're serious, aren't you?"

"*Jah*. Why?"

"Because I bet that half the girls I know would make me pay for that kiss with a dozen compliments or try to parlay it into a marriage proposal—" He broke off.

"I don't want anything from you, Joel Umble." Her voice was clear for all its quiet, and it resonated in his heart.

*I don't want anything from him, but that's a lie . . . I'm being selfish . . . Suppose he thinks that I might have feelings for him or that—that he might have feelings for me—He could get hurt in more ways than one when he finds out about Judah . . . and all because I'm a silly girl who doesn't want to give up my dreams . . .*

She stood up abruptly and felt his bewilderment even as she turned to face him.

"Martha—what? What's wrong?"

"Nothing, but you have to *geh*. Now. I—I was being foolish; a very silly girl."

He rose and trailed a finger down her shoulder, causing her to shiver with pleasure against her will. "You're a very beautiful woman."

She shook her head and walked away from him

to open the door, letting in the blustery cold air. "Please *geh.*"

He put his hat on in slow motion, then moved to pass her—but stopped and looked at her directly. "I told you once, Martha. I'm not giving up. I will not give up on us."

He stepped out into the dark *nacht*, and she closed the door, pulling the latch tight. *Us . . . Us . . . He's not giving up on us. But there is no us . . .*

And the reality of this thought caused her to sink to the icy floor beneath her bare feet and begin to sob.

# Chapter Eight

"Where was Judah last *nacht*, Joel?"

His mother's voice was worried as she served their breakfast of scrambled eggs, ham steak, and wheat toast.

"Probably out checking a trap," Joel said wearily. He'd noticed his *bruder* hadn't been abed the previous *nacht* but had been too focused on Martha to care. "And that's where he is this morning, too, I bet."

"I guess so." His *mamm* played with her toast, breaking it into small pieces, and Joel sighed, longing to ease the anxious movements of his mother's fingers.

"What was it like when Daed courted you? Can you tell me?"

His *mamm* stared at him, seeming almost startled by his abrupt question. Joel realized that in no way would an Amish woman of his mother's generation discuss courting with a *sohn*, but he was happy that he'd broken her anxious train of thoughts for a moment.

"Joel," she finally snapped. "How dare you ask such a question?"

He secretly delighted in the fact that her face held a healthy flush of color, and he reached across the table to catch one of her hands in his. "Mamm, I love you. I want you to have abundant life."

She pulled away from him and snatched up her plate, rising from the table. "You talk foolishness, Joel. As if there is such a thing on this earth as abundant life . . . Huh, if you understood true worry, then you would never say—" She broke off, dumping the plate in the sink, and Joel felt a deep disconsolation.

"I need some things from the store," his mother murmured, her anger gone, quicksilver as always.

"Let me check on the sheep first, and then I'll *geh*." He took his dishes to the sink and walked outside, feeling a cold within that matched that of the mountain's chill.

Martha tried to concentrate on the fact that she knew there were enough leftovers from the basket the previous evening for both her and her family to eat. But she had to get away from the cabin—from her memory of the *nacht* before—even if it was only for a brief time.

She quietly took down the cracked black pocketbook that was hidden behind the coffee can on the single shelf in the kitchen area. She undid the clasp and stared at the few coins inside: all the money that was left from her working last summer, cleaning cabins for the *Englisch* on the other side of the mountain. She knew she could get a large sweet onion for three cents from Sol Kauffman's store and decided she'd make a venison stew in the Dutch oven for the next day's food. She took the small change, put the pocketbook back, and slipped from the cabin while the rest of her family still slept.

She tried to pray as she hurried along the slushy paths that led to the heart of the community, and she found that her steps beat out a tattoo in her head . . . *I won't think about it. I won't think about it* . . . But then a hawk called, triumphant in snatching its prey, and she bit her lip as her mind replayed the scene of her first courting with Judah Umble.

She'd gone to sleep with the chill disappointment of having pushed Joel away and was still in a tearful lassitude when a bold knock sounded on the door of her room. She went to open it automatically, never stopping to think that no person had ever knocked at that door in all her time of sleeping in the pantry.

She'd stared up at Judah and hastily wiped at her eyes, not wanting him to see any weakness in her.

"I've *kumme* to court and I see that you are ill prepared, as one might expect." He reached a menacing finger out to knot itself in her loose hair, then shut the door behind him.

She backed away from his stone-cold eyes,

wrenching her hair from his grasp, regardless of the pulling pain in her scalp.

He brushed past her, and she was unable to help comparing Judah's unholy scent of slain animals with Joel's refreshing soap. But even in the seconds that this thought passed through her mind, Judah had already stripped off his coat and hat, throwing them casually on the bed and turning back to her.

Then she saw that he held a Bible in his hand, and fear licked at her consciousness with a dreadful tongue.

"Kneel," he said coldly.

She wet her lips, thinking desperately of the vulnerability of her sleeping family in the small rooms next door. *Dear* Gott, *what does he want of me . . .*

"Now."

She lowered herself cautiously to her knees on the floor before him, trying hard not to shake from the frigid floorboards.

He gave her an impassive look, then thumbed through the Bible with purposeful intent. He found the passage he sought and held the Book out to her. She took it with shaking hands.

"Read the thirteenth verse and then repeat it aloud."

Martha stared down helplessly at the array of letters in the dim candlelight. "I—I can't," she whispered finally.

He grabbed a handful of her long hair and nearly lifted her off the floor. Her eyes filled with silent tears.

"Read it," he hissed.

"I can't," she gasped, frantic not to cry out as he shook her. "I can't read."

Martha kicked disconsolately at an exposed pinecone, her eyes welling as she came back to the moment. She found that her heart was pounding with distress, and she was furious that Judah could so affect her, even when he was not present. She paused on the edge of the woods, taking a moment to compose herself before crossing the path to Sol Kauffman's general store. The store kept no regular business hours and was usually open from dawn until dusk except when closed on Sundays.

Martha steeled her resolve, lifted her head high, and walked out of the woods.

Sol Kauffman's store was the hubbub of social talk for the Ice Mountain Amish community. And there was no such thing as too early for a game of checkers or a chat around the woodstove or in the aisles.

Joel leaned against a back counter and listened to the sonorous snoring of the older-than-time Deacon Troyer, who was interrupted occasionally with grunts of appreciation by the onlookers when a proper move was made on the hand-carved checkerboard.

He idly saw women on the periphery, in the aisles, and at the dry goods counter and couldn't help but wonder what Martha was doing. *Probably caring for everyone at home but herself . . .* He realized instinctively that she was the type of person who would always put others before herself, yet she also knew how to refresh herself or have a bit of play—like bathing in the creek . . . The thought made him shift uncomfortably, and he almost jumped when Sol's normally booming voice came out softer and more gentle than usual.

"Wal now, Martha Yoder, what can I do fer ya this fine morning?"

Joel looked up to see Martha standing not more than five feet away, and he blinked at the vision she made even in a tattered cloak and slightly flattened bonnet.

"I'd like an onion," she murmured, and Joel wondered how a word so prosaic as "onion" could become beautiful when it came from her mouth.

She pulled her hands from beneath her cloak and laid three pennies on the counter.

"Here, let me," Joel said quickly, without thinking.

"*Nee, danki.*" She lifted her chin, and he realized he'd trespassed on her sense of pride—

and, more than that, Sol Kauffman was giving him a dirty look in case Joel might be scaring away a customer.

Joel moved to stand behind her, trying to focus on the checkers game while the fresh mountain scent of her teased and tantalized his senses. He watched Sol take the three pennies and hand her a small brown bag. She nodded her thanks and turned round, only to run smack dab into Joel, and he steadied her with hands that automatically sought the gentle curves of her waist for a moment.

Her eyes lifted to his, and he heard the question as if she had spoken it aloud. *What are you doing?*

He smiled and half shook his head, letting her go and stepping out of her way so that she might pass. He expected to follow her out of the store, but to his surprise, she paused at the dry goods counter where Sol's *dochder*, Lucy, did a brisk trade.

Joel watched the few other Amish women present move aside to speak in hushed tones as Martha began to gently finger the fabrics that were scrap yardage in an open basket on the counter. He watched her slender forefinger stroke a pink flannel, and he thought of how strong yet tender any *dochders* of hers would surely be. Then she touched black wool, and he swallowed, remembering her enveloped in his heavy coat. He also realized that she was touching the fabric textures for the sensory experience and that she appreciated beautiful things. But at the last piece of fabric displayed, he felt her hesitation as her hand hovered over a rich blue, and he realized that this was the color of a typical bride's dress for an Amish girl. Without thought, he let one of his hands lace over hers, and their fingertips brushed the blue together.

Martha half turned, clearly confused, and whispered in a strained tone, "What are you doing?"

"I'm courting you, Martha Yoder," he whispered back. "In broad daylight . . . You'd look beautiful in this shade of bridal blue. Do you know that?"

Her mouth tightened, and she practically wrenched her hand from his touch. "*Nee*," she gasped. "I don't know it and never will."

He watched her eyes fill with unshed tears, and he ached to hold her close, but she had turned away and was half an aisle away from him already.

He hurried after her, heedless of the women's inquisitive looks, and he reached the large store front door just as Martha did. He was surprised when its weight was pushed from the outside and Martha stepped back in the presence of Bishop Loftus, who was looking decidedly more grim than usual. Joel stood behind Martha as the bishop shut the door so that it rattled, and the store took on an ominous quiet.

"I fear I have bad news," the bishop intoned in his ringing sermon voice. "I've been up to the high timber and found that Dan Zook has been shot dead. I've also discovered the murderer . . ." For an eerie second, the bishop's shark-black eyes seemed to zone in on Joel's own, then moved on. "Stephen Lambert shot *auld* Dan, without a doubt."

Joel's head pounded at the accusation against his best friend and the apparent death of the beloved mountain man. Could this be the meaning of his strange vision when he was in the woods with Dan? He swallowed hard, then broke the silence. "How do you know Stephen Lambert was the one who did this?"

The shark eyes were back, boring into him. "Do you question me, Joel Umble?" The bishop's voice was deceptively soft, and Joel nodded, sensing Martha's tension as she stood in front of him.

"*Jah*, I question, as we all should, to be very sure of who could have done this to Dan."

The bishop turned away from him. "Of course you want to protect your friend—commendable. But there will be a meeting at the school*haus* in one hour to question Lambert himself. And then burial preparations must be made for Dan Zook.

Being shunned, he cannot be buried in the local Amish cemetery, of course."

Joel felt a red haze burn behind his eyelids, and he had to restrain himself from actually laying hands on the *aulder* man. He was about to speak up when Martha's voice came out clear and true, even though it was absolutely not a woman's place to speak in that moment.

"*Auld* Dan Zook was a *gut* man. Many has been the time he's fed my family. He would want to be buried in the high timber, where he loved to live."

"Silence!" the bishop hissed. "How dare you, woman? Get thee home to tend your family and pray that nothing worse befalls your *haus* because of your wicked tongue."

Joel watched Martha hurry out, and then he gave Bishop Loftus a cold glare. "What Martha Yoder spoke was truth, not wickedness, and I begin to question whether you are always able to discern the difference."

The bishop gobbled wordlessly; then Joel, too, quit the ugly tension of the store.

# Chapter Nine

Martha heard Joel calling her name but she ran on, as fleet as a doe, trying to lose him in the myriad paths of the forest. Nonetheless, he caught up with her, and she didn't bother to hide her sobs.

"Martha, don't cry. What the bishop says is not worth your tears." He gently took her forearms in his large hands and stroked the skin revealed by her dress.

She shook her head. "*Nee*, I endangered my family because of my impulsive words."

She felt him lean in close, his blue eyes dark in their intensity. "Martha, no evil can come from speaking the truth. The bishop was only trying to frighten you."

"I know that, and I know *Gott* gives us the truth, but Bishop Loftus has the power to shun, and that means starvation and—" She broke off, realizing she'd said too much.

"Do you think, as long as I have breath in my body, that I'd ever let you starve?" He pulled her closer. "And I don't care if you decide to court me or not. I'd never let that happen."

She felt more tears fall afresh when she thought of Dan Zook. "*Auld* Dan—he fed us."

Joel nodded. "I know."

Then she thought of something. "Joel, I think I'd feel right if gentle hands prepared him for burial, and more than that, perhaps if we—I mean you—went to his cabin, you might find something to prove Stephen's innocence."

He caught her hand in his and took her bag from her. "We'll drop the onion off at your *haus* and tell them where we'll be, but we'll have to hurry. I think the bishop is allowing only an hour until the meeting at the school*haus* so that no one can do anything to help Stephen."

"But why Stephen? Why accuse him?" she asked as they began to run along the trail.

"I don't know, but as you say, maybe we can find out."

Martha hurried beside him and couldn't prevent the feeling of warmth inside of her that he valued her words and ideas highly enough to act on them.

Joel was unprepared for the rush of emotion he felt when they reached Dan Zook's cabin. He realized that he was probably in shock . . . He found the small place to be the picture of neatness, and the ax in the log outside and the hide tanning in the wind each bore testament to a life interrupted. But Joel understood that, murder or not, *Gott* knew when it was a person's time to die, and this brought him a measure of comfort.

"Should we *geh* in?" Martha asked gently, and

he felt her studying him as he swiped a hand across his eyes.

"*Jah*. But I'll take a look first, if you don't mind."

She smiled sadly at him. "There are worse things to look upon in life than death itself. Please don't worry for me."

He nodded, once more admiring her inner strength and purpose.

They walked forward, and Joel eased open the door. The scent of blood drifted to him, and he saw Dan lying in his bunk, seemingly peaceful but for the wounds in his chest and the blood splattered nearby.

"Shotgun." Joel murmured the grim fact. "He was probably asleep when he was killed."

He felt Martha's steady presence beside him and then went to kneel beside the body of his *auld* friend. "Maybe—maybe I might have prevented this," he choked out.

He felt Martha touch his shoulder. "What do you mean?"

"I know I sound *narrish*, but—the last time I saw Dan, I saw sort of a . . . vision . . . of death and blood and—"

"You have the second sight. That's all." Her clear voice was calm, and he half turned to look up at her.

"The—second sight?"

"My grandmother speaks of it at times. It's a

gift, Joel Umble, even if it means seeing things as hard as this." Her slender fingers tightened on his shoulder, and he turned back to Dan's body.

"I know Stephen like I know myself," Joel whispered. "He couldn't have done this."

"Do you think Bishop Loftus will contact the *Englisch* authorities?"

Joel shook his head. "*Nee*, he's too arrogant a man. And you know things tend to be handled among us without outsiders. Stephen will be shunned . . . That will be deemed punishment enough."

"As Dan was shunned . . ." she murmured, and he felt the gentle firmness of her fingers move to stroke the back of his neck.

"*Jah*," he whispered, bowing his head for a moment as he felt for one of his *auld* friend's big, cold hands. "Like Dan . . ."

Martha moved to help Joel wrap Dan's body in the bedclothes that surrounded him, but as she lifted the edge of the patchwork quilt, something thudded heavily to the floor at her feet. She bent down and picked up the black Bible, automatically handing it to Joel.

He paused, and she watched him look down at the inside flap and then flip through the pages. "It must be Dan's. There's no name inside—not that that's unusual."

"But Dan's Bible is here." She indicated the

small bedside table. "He told me once that he used colored threads to mark his favorite passages." She thought for a moment. "Perhaps that one belongs to Dan's murderer."

"*Jah*," Joel said slowly. "It's possible." She watched him slip the Bible into his coat pocket, and then he bent to help her finish their ministrations to Dan's body.

The school*haus* was crowded with the Amish men of the community. Joel arrived in time to stand far in the back of the small room and saw that Stephen stood hatless and grim at the front, near the teacher's desk and behind Bishop Loftus. Judah seemed to be nowhere, and Joel had the brief thought that his *bruder*'s absence seemed odd, but then he was consumed by the tension around him. There was an air of suppressed excitement among those gathered, and Joel could feel it. *Like some crazed hex hunt* . . . He reined in his thoughts as Bishop Loftus began to speak.

"We are here to discuss the murder of Dan Zook. Although he lived under the *bann*, he was still a brother. A brother killed by another of us. I myself saw Stephen Lambert near the path that leads from Dan's cabin. And he looked like this . . ."

The bishop gestured to Stephen, who opened his black coat with a defiant air. His white shirt and suspenders were covered in blood. There was a rumbling among those watching.

Joel frowned heavily and elbowed through the throng until he was halfway up the school aisle. Then he met Stephen's gaze and knew once more the strange chasm of thought and vision that had opened before him that *nacht* in the woods with Dan. He saw Stephen bent over the lifeless form of a deer, seeming to work frantically with a knife . . . *But Dan was killed with a shotgun . . .* His thoughts became a futile cry as the crowd of men gathered gave low-voiced consent to whatever sentence Bishop Loftus seemed to have pronounced. Joel caught hold of the man nearest him—Abe Mast. "What did he say? What did the bishop decide?"

Abe frowned behind his thick beard. "Quiet down, Joel Umble. The *gut* bishop said that Lambert is shunned and charged with the burying of ole Dan. The *buwe*'s getting off easy, if you ask me."

Joel watched as Stephen exited the building through the back door, followed by a solemn silence. Joel wanted to scream, to tell what he knew to be truth, but he also knew how he might better serve his best friend and turned to head home for a shovel.

Martha returned home from Dan's cabin with a prayer in her heart for Joel. She knew that he had been distracted and grave, except when he'd given her a warm, hard kiss goodbye.

She shivered with pleasure at the thought and mounted the rickety steps to her family's cabin. Immediately upon entering, she caught the smell of pretzel and potato soup—something she could recall from childhood.

"Grossmuder—who's been here?" Martha indicated the shiny kettle on the fire—definitely not belonging to them.

Her grandmother rolled a baleful eye. "Anne Mast *kumme* with the soup, but what she really wanted was a nasty piece of gossip—about you, dearie."

Martha stopped short. "About me?" Then realization dawned . . . *My words in Sol Kauffman's store to the bishop are already being bandied about.* "*Ach*." She lowered her voice. "Did she speak to Mamm and Daed?"

"A lot more than she talked to me . . . And I tried her soup . . . Hah, the pretzels were that much soggy."

Martha smiled faintly, then took slow steps to her parents' room.

Her mother was sitting up, and Martha looked at her with concern. "Mamm . . . Daed . . . are you both well at the moment?"

"As well as one can be, Dochder, after drinking mushy soup." Her *daed*'s snort of disdain made Martha breathe a sigh of relief.

"Not that we shouldn't be grateful for the soup," her *mamm* said softly. "It's the gossip that stirs me."

"*Jah*." Martha's *fater* roused himself upright for a brief moment. "Gossip and lies. Saying that our *maedel* would speak so to the bishop, of all folks."

Martha drew a deep breath then voiced the truth. "It is as she says, Fater. I—I wanted to defend Dan Zook, and I spoke before I thought."

"As if the dead need defending, girl. Could you not have held your tongue?" Her *fater*'s tone was mild and hurt her more than if he'd been outright angry.

A vivid image of Judah passed through Martha's mind, and she shivered. *Joel may promise never to let us starve, but what of Judah? He'd probably be the first to burn the potato bin . . .*

She went and knelt by her *daed*'s bedside and looked into his brown eyes, weary with pain. "I'm sorry, Fater. I will guard my tongue in the future."

"*Nee*, you won't, and we should be thankful that the girlie's got some spirit!" Her *grossmuder*'s voice echoed from the next room.

Martha had to smile. There was little wrong with her grandmother's hearing, despite her advanced age. Martha glanced back to her *fater*'s face and smothered a sigh when she saw his eyes—distracted and distant.

"Went huntin' with Eli Loftus once, before he was bishop . . . It was when his wife was still alive. He asked me back to his cabin for lunch, and I figured I'd *geh*. We got there, but Violet had run to the store. He was furious . . . I tried to brush it off and take him for lunch to our place, but the anger had already got hold of him. He took the big canister of flour from the shelf and set it down on the floor, then he kicked it hard. The lid clanked off and flour flew everywhere about the cabin—a ghostly mess. Then he turns to me and says, 'There. That'll teach her not to have better things to do when I'm wanting lunch.' I just stared at him, sorry for Violet, silenced by his evilness. I know she surely must have found peace in death."

Martha swallowed hard and caught her *fater*'s right hand close.

"He's still that cruel man, Dochder. Don't forget . . ."

"I won't, Daed." She blinked back tears. "I won't."

Joel struck the muddy ground with his shovel and glanced sideways at Stephen.

"What are you doing, Joel? You heard it. I'm under the *bann*, and you will be, too, if anyone sees us together."

"It's a risk I'm willing to take."

"Well, I'm not worth it," Stephen said flatly.

Joel stopped and laid a hand on Stephen's bloodstained sleeve. "What really happened? I know this isn't Dan's blood." He wondered briefly if he should tell Stephen of the vision he'd had at the school*haus*, but his friend was speaking . . .

"*Nee*, it isn't Dan's." Stephen shrugged, then swallowed hard. "I was up here walking, even thinking about visiting Dan. But then I heard something kicking about in the brush, and I went to take a look. It was a doe—bad shot by a poacher most likely. I had to take her life, but she was pregnant, and I'd hoped to save the fawn but wasn't able to—Bishop Loftus caught me walking away a few hundred feet down the mountain, then hauled me down to the school*haus*. And that's all."

Joel remembered seeing the image of Stephen and the deer and resisted the eerie feeling that raced along his spine. *The second sight* . . . "Why didn't you tell him the truth?"

Stephen shook his dark head tiredly. "Practically the first words out of his mouth were about killing Dan, shunning me and mine, and I couldn't take the risk of involving my *mamm* or her sister . . . so, I—went along."

Joel thrust the shovel into the ground. "We're going to *geh* talk to Loftus."

"*Nee*, we're not. Let it be, Joel. You know things aren't great with *mamm* at home. I—I'm going to stay here in Dan's cabin and make my way. I'll get food down to my *mamm* and *aenti* at *nacht*. I'm sorry I won't be able to help you on the farm."

Joel blew out a hot breath. "This isn't right— that man's got you running scared. He has a lot of folks in his grip, and I don't like it. I'm going to see Deacon Troyer . . ."

Stephen half smiled. "He's so *auld*, he won't be able to hear you."

"How can you joke?"

"Because on Ice Mountain, what the bishop says is law. Truth doesn't have a place here anymore."

"Well, it's going to," Joel said grimly. "Some-how, things have to be put right."

Stephen caught him in a brief hug. "*Derr Herr* must see to that, Joel Umble—not you."

Joel nodded and worked in silence with Stephen for the next hour, digging the grave of their lost friend.

# Chapter Ten

Late that afternoon, Martha heard the echoing sound of an ax as she tucked her *mamm* up more comfortably.

"Someone's cutting wood for us," her mother murmured. "A blessing."

"*Jah*, Mamm," Martha responded in soft tones, though her heart had begun to gallop in her chest. *Could it be Judah? But* nee, *he would be unlikely to put himself out doing extra work for my family* . . . Still, she slipped into the small pantry and out the side door of her room, the better to safely see who it was that was working the craggy wood knots she'd managed to gather the previous fall.

She recognized Joel's tall form, his light blue shirt clinging damply to his broad back, and she hurried to draw a fresh bucket of water from the well, then approached him, watching as he swung the ax with ruthless precision.

When she took another step closer, he stopped and turned to look at her, then swiped a dirty arm across his forehead. She could see that his blue eyes were stark with both anger and grief.

"How is Stephen?" she asked softly.

He swallowed hard. "As well as can be

expected . . . The bishop shunned him and then ordered him to bury Dan."

She reached and touched a dirt smudge on his right arm. "And you went to help?"

"Stephen's been my friend since we were *kinner* . . ." He shook his dark head. "There was little else I could do."

She set the wooden bucket of water on the ground at his feet. "Of course you had to . . ." She stooped and dipped the hem of her dress into the cold well water, then rose to her feet. She lifted her dress and began to wipe at the mud on his face.

"*Ach*, Martha . . ." he whispered, and turned so that his lips found the inside of her outstretched wrist. It was difficult for her to concentrate, but then he pulled back, and she found the fine bone structure of his cheeks and forehead. He closed his eyes, his lashes lying in thick, dark crescents against his flushed skin, his lips parted as she trailed the cloth over the firmness of his mouth. His breathing became ragged, and she couldn't resist dropping the hem of her dress and raising herself on tiptoe to press her lips against his own. And it was as if he stood spellbound, letting her explore with tender grace the shape of his mouth.

She vaguely heard the ax fall from his hand with a dull thud, and then he was kissing her in return. She smelled earth and something like the spring wind as he slid his hands up to cup her face. "Dear *Gott* . . . you're sweet."

She shivered with pleasure when he ran his tongue against the seam of her lips. She looked up and his eyes were open, rich blue, the pupils huge. Slowly, she opened her mouth to the demand of his seeking tongue and then savored his sweet breath as they kissed, tasting each other. She knew a burning ache in her breasts and instinctively nestled closer to him, seeking some kind of relief to the teasing pleasure-pain she felt.

Then she suddenly became aware that they were kissing in the broad light of day and that Judah could *kumme* around at any time. She wrenched herself from Joel, and he almost staggered forward. "Martha, what—" he gasped.

"I'm sorry, Joel. It's not that I don't want your mouth and your mind . . . and all of you . . . but right here . . . before my parents' home . . ." She struggled for words.

He visibly came to himself by slow degrees, then nodded in agreement. "*Jah* . . . your home. I'd better *geh*, Martha . . . I'm sorry that I lost control." He bent and picked up the ax, then grabbed his coat from the old log.

Martha pressed her hands together in sudden uncertainty, wondering if she'd put him off for good, when he turned and bent to swipe her cheek with a quick kiss. "I'll still *kumme* to court tonight, if it's all right?"

She nodded before she could help herself, then watched him stalk off through the newly budding trees while she prayed that Judah would not come to her that *nacht*.

Joel decided to bathe in the icy creek that ran past the back of his family's property. It would cool both his body and his blood. Kissing Martha was as heady as drinking dandelion wine and twice as sweet. He could hardly wait until the evening . . .

He stripped down and was about to take the first mind-numbing plunge when a pitiful sound reached him through the rush of the water. He scanned the opposite bank and groaned aloud when he saw his sheep, Lost Lenore, floundering against some rocks.

He slid into the water and concentrated on speaking in loud but calm tones to the ewe, not wanting her to spook and be lost downstream. It was miraculous that she'd managed to hang on in full wool.

He made his way across and got close to her, but her soaking wool was pulling her under, and once she saw him, her movements increased frantically.

He knew she probably weighed close to two hundred pounds and it would take all he had to get her out. *But they that wait upon the Lord shall find new strength . . . New strength,* Derr Herr, *please . . .* The Scripture floated through his mind as he grasped Lenore and tried to haul her out of the current and onto the higher bank.

Clearly terrified, she bucked her rear legs and caught him square in the chest. Out of breath, he heaved Lenore once more toward a foothold, but only ended up moving her a few inches. His bare feet were cut on the churning rocks of the creek bottom, but he pressed on and finally got her clear of the water. Once on solid ground, the ewe scrabbled to her feet, then balefully cried out to him as he staggered from the creek.

He was gasping and slicked his hair back from his face only to hear the sound of crude laughter. He recognized his *bruder*'s voice and bit the inside of his mouth to keep from commenting as he slowly made his way to sit naked on the ground while Lenore pressed her wet body against his side.

"*Ach*, Joel, you really are a sight, yet you'll sit there freezing for that stupid sheep without anything to show for it."

A rough towel hit Joel on the side of the head, and he snatched it away to start rubbing Lenore down.

"The towel was for you, little *bruder*."

"Should I be grateful then?" Joel bit out, the cold starting to get to him.

"You should be." Judah's tone was mocking, even over the sound of the creek, and Joel knew a sudden and frightening urge to strike his brother.

*Over a simple exchange . . . what is wrong with me? I can usually handle Judah fine . . .*

But the feeling persisted, and Joel used the warmth of his anger to haul himself to his feet and focus on crossing the log footbridge back to where his clothes lay. He pulled on his pants and watched Judah warily out of the corner of his eye. Lenore had abandoned him and run back to the barn, and Joel planned on getting into the *haus* to tend his feet before any more conflict with Judah could occur. But his older *bruder* seemed to want to toy with him and followed him into the cabin making hurtful remarks.

At supper that *nacht*, Joel broke his bread and tried to put aside Judah's malice, but it wasn't easy.

"I'll be leaving tomorrow at first light to check my traplines," Judah announced when their mother had served the chocolate sheet cake she'd made for dessert.

"*Ach*, Judah, must you?" she implored, and Joel felt a surge of impatience when his *bruder* grinned at him across the table.

"Joel will keep you safe enough, Mamm . . . or at least he can try. I'll only be gone three days."

"Mamm and I will be fine, Judah. You *geh* and do your work—such as it is."

Joel felt even more startled inside than Judah looked. It was almost funny—almost. He rarely, if ever, was moved past irritation with Judah, yet here he was, deliberately serving insults with the chocolate frosting and actually feeling *gut* about it in the process. Fortunately, Joel caught sight of their mother's strained and anxious face, and all anger left him. But the situation was eerie and left Joel feeling cold inside; he counted the hours until he might gain warmth from Martha.

Martha finished her evening chores and saw to it that everyone was tucked in and then fast asleep. She hastened to her room and set the tiny place to rights before sitting down nervously on the edge of her bed—waiting and praying, and still fully dressed, with her hair properly *kapp*ed. The moonlight stretched long fingers across the floor and up her legs, and she almost fell asleep, but then jerked herself back to attention. *Perhaps neither Joel nor Judah will* kumme *this* nacht *after all.*

She lay down stiffly on her hay-filled mattress, only to be startled into alertness by a bold knock on her door. She knew instinctively that it was Judah, and her throat constricted with fear. Still, she forced herself to stand and cross the floor, opening the door before he might knock again and disturb her family . . .

# Chapter Eleven

Judah entered without preamble, pushing past her to take his coat off and throw it carelessly on the foot of the bed.

"Lie down," he ordered, his eyes glittering. She felt her heart begin to gallop at his command but knew she must be silent. She thought of protesting and decided it would probably only provoke him more. *Yet, to rape me in my own bed, I—*

"Hurry," he growled and she lay down with her hands fisted at her sides. She longed to close her eyes but stared up at him instead as he seemed to tower over her.

"Have you no bundling board?" he asked after a long moment, and she drew a sudden breath of reprieve.

"There—there are some pieces of wood beneath the overhang outside."

He nodded and jerked the frail door open.

Martha shuddered and forced herself to slow her breathing. She knew that bundling was a time-honored tradition in her Amish world. Sometimes called bed courtship, it had originated as a means to keep courting couples warm. Martha had heard her *grossmuder* speak about how her own suitor had to be sewn in a long sack

91

to prevent any intimacy. But now, bundling had become a way for courting couples to share time together and to talk in whispers while getting to know each other better.

Judah returned with a long, jagged board, which he pressed hard against Martha's side and legs. "This will serve," he growled. "And I am sure that I will be safe from any temptation so long as you invoke no witchcraft."

"I am no hex, Judah," she said before thinking. He lay down on his side facing her and reached a casual hand up to jerk with savagery at her *kapp*. The pins caught in her hair, and she had to blink back tears at the sudden pain.

Judah flung the white *kapp* to the bottom of the bed, then grabbed her shoulder until she was forced to turn on her side, face-to-face with him. She bit her lip and made herself stare into his brown eyes. There was almost a dullness in them, as if he truly were spellbound, and she knew that pleading with him would make no difference.

"Not a hex, hmmm? The *gut* Bishop Loftus warned that you would say that."

"The . . . bishop?" she stuttered in surprise, feeling as though something slimy had crawled down her back. "You've talked of me with the bishop?"

He caught her fragile jaw in his cruel grasp. "How dare you question me? You are wicked and a hex, but it is my task to save you."

"*Nee*, Judah—we can none of us save ourselves or others. Even our breath is *Gott*-given. Surely you realize this."

"We will see, hex . . . Let us examine your breath for what it is."

She tried to press her back against the wall behind her, instinctively wanting to elude his hands, but the bundling board proved no impediment as he released her jaw only to move both hands now to the slender outline of her throat.

"Your heart beats like a wild rabbit's," he murmured as she reached her own hands up to try and claw at his fingers, but he merely tightened his grasp.

"Judah," she gasped. "Think . . . please."

He smiled, and she knew he was beyond any rational thought. He began to choke her, and she felt growing pain that burned her lungs and throat in merciless waves until everything dissolved into one black and blessed center.

Joel found his way through the dark forest, then was led by the faint glimmer of a guttering candle shining from what he thought was Martha's window. He soon realized, though, that the candle shone through her open door, which hung forlornly in the *nacht* wind.

He entered with a cautious knock, instinctively feeling that something was wrong.

"Martha?"

At first he thought she lay deeply asleep as the candlelight threw eerie shadows over her bed. But as he stepped closer, his mind registered several things at once: She didn't appear to be breathing, her clothes were disheveled, and an apparent bundling board lay jagged and cruel against her inert form.

He laid the board aside, then put his hand on her chest and mercifully found her to be alive. "*Ach* . . . praise *Derr Herr*." He lifted her into his arms and put his mouth against her throat, letting his lips feel her pulse. Then he ran out into the *nacht*, knowing that he had to get Martha to the healer.

He prayed as he ran and soon gained May's cottage on its steep hill. The door was opened before he could even knock.

"In here." May led the way to an adjacent bedroom, and Joel laid Martha down with gentle hands. May turned up the kerosene lamp, and Joel stared with sudden horror at the bruises on Martha's throat.

"I—I couldn't see this before." He reached tender fingers to brush against the marred skin.

"Joel. I think you'd better *geh* out. Fetch me a bucket of fresh water from the well and I'll call you when—in a few minutes."

Joel nodded and stalked from the small bedroom, automatically reaching for the bucket, even as his mind burned with the image of Martha's abused throat.

Martha heard the gentle persistence of the feminine voice calling her name. But sleep seemed so much more pleasant, and she was reluctant to leave the cocoon of warmth that surrounded her mind.

But finally, she came awake to find herself in a strange but comfortable bed and looked up to see May Miller's placid face above her.

"Can you speak, Martha?"

It seemed an odd request, but then the horror of Judah choking her came back in a frightful rush. She opened her mouth and tried to speak, only nothing came out but a raspy whisper.

Still, May smiled down at her as if satisfied. "Your voice will improve; the vocal cords have not been permanently damaged."

Martha nodded, but she was still afraid that she might never regain her voice and, worse still, she had no recollection of what Judah might have done to her once she'd become unconscious. As if reading her thoughts, May spoke softly.

"Did he rape you?"

Martha felt her eyes widen, and she choked on a hoarse breath. "I—I don't—"

May nodded. "Will you say his name? The one who did this to you . . . ?"

*Will I say his name? Will I name Judah as the*

*sick man he is even while he courts the bishop's favor—and they both think I'm a hex . . . Will I say his name when it will cut Joel to the quick and wound his family forever?*

Tears fell unbidden down her cheeks, and May gently wiped them away. "We will talk again later. But Joel waits to see you. He carried you here."

Martha wet her lips and nodded briefly. Part of her wanted to push Joel away and never see him again, but only because she wanted to keep him safe. Yet she knew that she had to look at least once more into his dark blue eyes . . .

"Martha?"

She turned her head to stare at him as he quietly entered the room. He wore no hat or coat, and his long burgundy sleeves were rolled up to his elbows. As he neared the bed and dropped to his knees beside her, she saw a dark brown stubble on his jaw that made him look all the more appealing.

"Don't try to talk," he said soothingly. She liked the sound of his voice and knew it to be one that might easily calm a child. *He would make a* gut fater . . . She blinked back fresh tears at the thought and felt him reach for her right hand atop the bed quilts. She squeezed his strong fingers and longed to tell him how much she loved him.

Then, suddenly, she saw his body tense, and

his facial features appeared stricken, as if he'd seen some ghostly apparition. She knew he was having a vision of some sort, and she prayed as she waited and watched the color drain from his face.

Joel tried to focus on Martha's face and then her eyes but the world seemed to slip away from him in a dissolving rush. *I don't want this—this second sight.* He cried out the words in a silent scream. But then there was Judah, skinning a wolf, setting traps for innocents, and laying cruel hands on Martha's throat. He felt the pressure in his lungs, the gasping for air only to know that no relief was coming. He saw his *bruder* loom over Martha, his gaze lewd and vile, but then Judah turned and ran out into the concealment of the *nacht* . . .

Joel came back to himself, his breathing forced and labored as he stared into Martha's worried eyes.

"Joel?" she questioned tentatively.

"*Jah.*"

"Is everything all right?"

He heard the effort it took for her to get the words out, and he nodded while pressing her hand. "*Jah* . . . I'm going to kill Judah."

Martha saw the resolute intent in Joel's eyes. She wanted to say something, to tell him *nee*, but then

May bustled into the room with a wooden tray. She sat down on the edge of the bed opposite Joel, and Martha reluctantly accepted the spoonfuls of honeyed tea that May began to give her.

"So it's murder you're speaking of, Joel Umble? Murder, and you an Amish man?" May's voice was soft, but her message was pointed.

Martha watched Joel struggle with his anger, but then he lifted his head, and there was a light in his blue eyes. He smiled at her; a tender smile that made her shift her legs restlessly beneath the quilts.

"Judah is gone for three days checking his traps," Joel began.

Martha nodded.

"And there is one way that I might protect you other than laying hands on my *bruder*." He let his clever fingers play along the inside of her wrist, seeming to ignore May's presence. "I'm already on both knees, Martha Yoder. Will you marry me?"

"Well," May said dryly, clattering the spoon in the teacup. "I think that's my cue to leave you two alone."

Martha turned her head to watch May leave the small room and then looked back at Joel. "You don't know what you're asking," she whispered, then shrugged helplessly. "My family . . ."

". . . will become my family too." He bent to press his lips against the pulse point in her wrist.

"And . . . Judah?"

He lifted his dark head and stared at her. "Judah is in league, no doubt, with Bishop Loftus, who would never consent to marry us. But you know that the bishop must recognize an *Englisch* writ of marriage and has done so for at least a few couples in the past. We will *geh* into Coudersport and wed. Judah will, I believe, leave the area once I've had words with him—especially when he realizes that you and I are sealed in marriage."

She swept her lashes downward, wondering what it would be to have Joel Umble as a husband. *And yet there are so many reasons why it might not work—my poverty, the drain my family will be on body and soul, our differences in schooling* . . . She knew she should protest his plan, but a small part of her heart, a kindled flame, wanted very badly to try.

"Martha—" He called her back to the moment with gentle tones, and she nodded.

"*Jah*, Joel. I'll marry you."

# Chapter Twelve

Joel had arranged for May to watch over both Martha's family and his own mother for one day and *nacht*. He'd spent half the morning trying to be casual with his *mamm* about his trip to Coudersport. He didn't want to lie to her but knew that she'd tell Judah if she discovered his intended marriage—and if Judah should return early from checking traps.

"They're experimenting now, Mamm, with a nutrient, selenium, to aid in the diet of ewes about to give birth. I'd like to lay my hands on some, if the research is right."

"*Ach*, Joel, always reading, you are! Why not wait until Judah returns? You know how I hate to be alone."

"I understand," he'd said soothingly. "But May the healer is coming to visit, and spring is almost upon us, and you know that means lambing season."

He'd finally persuaded her, then gathered a few things in a satchel, along with some items from Sol Kauffman's store, and headed to Martha's. He had marrying on his mind, but not before he spoke to Martha's *fater*. It was not always customary that the potential groom ask for the *fater*'s permission to marry, but Joel felt in his spirit that it was the right thing to do and knew also that Martha's family would keep their silence until the marriage had been accomplished.

He knocked on the cabin's door and was not surprised when Martha opened it, though the sight of the black kerchief round her neck brought back a rushing surge of anger.

"Are you able to be up?" he asked low. "I'm not sure we shouldn't wait another day to hike—"

"Joel, I'm all right."

He noted that her voice was stronger, and he stepped closer to her, longing to kiss her once and hard. But Esther Yoder's delicate laugh brought him to his senses.

He had to smile as Martha widened the door and her *grossmuder* greeted him with kindness. "*Ach*, so it's the strong man again. *Kumme* for my girlie, have you?"

Joel glanced at Martha, unsure of what she might have told her *grossmuder*, but the *auld* woman laughed again. "I'll wager it's my son-in-law yer wantin' to talk with. He's in the other room, as if ya don't already know." There was a subtle play in the woman's words that caught at Joel's senses and made his heart beat fast. *What do I know? About the future, the past? What will Chet Yoder say when I ask him for his* dochder? *Her hand—her life? Am I ready for—*

"What can we do fer ya, *buwe*?"

Somehow, Joel had walked into the bedroom

101

and now stood staring down into eyes that had seen much pain but still shone with something to give. Joel didn't feel right towering over his potential *fater*-in-law so he dropped easily to the floor to sit beside the bed. Martha's *mamm* appeared to be sleeping, and he blew out a quick breath before beginning the words he'd rehearsed in the back of his mind—but Chet forestalled him with a raised, rugged hand.

"Tell me why it is, *buwe*, that the muskrats know to build their domes thicker when a bad winter's comin'?"

Joel blinked but the *aulder* man went on inexorably. "Tell me if the panther still roams these woods? Why is a mother bear so fierce in protecting her cubs? Why does the raven not flee the ice? Tell me what you know about logging and the river that runs to the sea." Chet stopped suddenly for breath, and the quietness in the small room was palpable.

Joel cleared his throat, feeling unaccountable tears in his eyes. "You know more than I ever will, sir. I understand what you are saying. Martha is part of this mountain, and the wild things that live here too. I will fiercely guard and protect her, Herr Yoder—you have my word on that—if . . . *ach*, if only you would allow her to become my wife."

"It is not our way for you ta be askin' me . . . but I appreciate the favor, *sohn*. You have my blessings. *Geh*." The conversation seemed to have cost the older man his strength, and Joel got to his feet, then turned to see Martha's *mamm* holding him softly with her eyes. He crossed the room and bent to kiss her cheek, which was as soft as rose petals, despite her illness.

"*Geh* with peace, Joel Umble," she whispered.

He smiled down at her. "It is a true pleasure to have another *mamm* in my life."

"And a *sohn* in mine."

He nodded, then looked to see Martha standing in the doorway. Her brown eyes were luminous, and he felt a surety in his soul that what they were about to do was right.

Martha wiggled her toes experimentally inside the new black stockings and found them to be delightfully warm. She glanced up at Joel from where she sat on the edge of her bed. He had begged for a few moments of privacy in her pantry room and had opened his satchel to produce the stockings and a new pair of black shoes.

"*Danki*," Martha said shyly. "But you don't have to do things like this." Then she met his gaze straight on. "I'm not going to marry you for—"

"My money?" he finished, and she felt herself flush but kept her eyes steady.

"*Jah*."

"Our money, Martha. The money and lands that I inherited from my earthly *daed* and the blessings from my Heavenly Fater—they are my pleasure to share." He bent his long legs to stoop before her and put his hands on either side of her hips.

She liked how his voice deepened as he seemed to savor the word "share." It made her shiver with delight, and she waited, thinking he might kiss her. But instead he gently fingered the kerchief round her neck.

"You need the shoes to hike down to the Ice Mine, but are you sure you can? How do you feel?"

She shook her head slightly as his dark hair brushed her cheek and couldn't think of anything much but his nearness. "I'm . . . fine."

"*Ach*, you are more than fine, Martha, and I would like to explore that point with you further, but the day is getting away from us." He kissed her quickly on her nose and got to his feet. She sighed to herself, wishing for more attention from his mouth.

They bid goodbye to her family and had started out when Joel glanced at the brief shawl she wore and shook his head. "Here, put my coat on."

"You'll be cold," she protested.

"And you're not?" There was an edge to his voice. "Look, Martha—I'd like to march you into Sol Kauffman's and buy you a whole new wardrobe—coat included. But I don't want to attract attention to us. So, we'll shop in Coudersport, and in the meantime, you'll wear this." He slid his warm coat around her shoulders, and she couldn't help but remember how he'd carried her shivering body home wrapped in black wool.

"I'll wear it, Joel Umble, but only if we might repeat—uh—" She floundered a bit, but he must have taken her meaning.

He bent to caress her cheek with his mouth, snuggling his coat a bit closer around her shoulders. Then he trailed his lips behind her ear and languidly sucked on her right earlobe, making her feel the alternate heat of his mouth and then the rushing chill of the air. Her mouth burned for want of him, but he teased her senses.

"How do you know how to do this—I mean, without ever having kissed before?" she asked on a partial gasp as his hands skimmed her waist, then moved a bit higher beneath the coat to press at her tingling belly.

She felt him smile against her cheek; then he pulled back to hover a bare inch from her lips. "Instinct, perhaps . . ." he whispered.

She almost raised on tiptoe to meet him but something caught at her awareness, and she turned round to see a young Amish *buwe* staring at them in fascination. "Joel." She pulled from him and watched his blue eyes narrow, then focus on the lad.

"Jared Mast, out and about, are you?" he asked after a moment.

The ruddy-faced child nodded. "You two were kissin' up a storm."

"So we were," Joel agreed. "But it's not to be widely known. So I'd ask you, man to man, if you'd protect a *maedel*'s privacy and not repeat what you've seen here."

"You mean not tell anybody?" The *buwe*'s pug nose tilted in suspicion, and Martha wet her lips, wondering if the child might run and tell the whole of the community.

But Joel's voice was steady and kind. "*Jah*, not tell for honor's sake."

"Huh?"

"To be honorable."

Jared shrugged his small shoulders. "*Jah*, I guess I won't."

"*Gut.*" Martha felt Joel pull from her to *geh* and extend a hand to Jared. "Let's shake on it then, like real men."

Jared opened his mouth in surprise, then held out his right hand. "I promise," the little fellow said clearly.

Martha watched Joel's smile in profile and felt a renewed kindling in her heart. *He's not only beautiful, but he's gut and kind too . . . Ach, Gott have mercy on us in what we do . . .*

106

Joel turned back to her as Jared scampered away through the melting snow.

"He might say something in passing," she murmured, still feeling a bit worried.

"We'll be married by then, Martha, even if he does. So let's take the little one at his word and count on *Derr Herr* for peace. All right?" He bent and kissed her mouth, and all else was lost in the tumult of her heartbeat and the heat of his nearness.

# Chapter Thirteen

The trek down the sodden path was treacherous with muddy, exposed roots and still-slippery patches of snow. However, Joel was happy when Martha pointed out the blooming lavender crocuses and yellow-throated snow flowers that persevered despite the cold and grew on the mountainside.

"Beauty in difficult circumstances," she murmured, indicating the flowers.

"Can I say that you rival their beauty, and you've definitely grown in difficult times."

She smiled sideways at him from beneath the fringe of her weather-beaten bonnet and he felt his heart warm.

"Do the boots fit all right?"

"Like a fine lady's glove." She laughed. "How did you know my size?"

He shrugged and squeezed her hand, not wanting to admit that he admired her slender feet and had studied her trim ankles on more than one occasion. "Just a guess."

She sighed and nodded. "Are you sure, Joel Umble, that this is a *gut* idea? You've barely had time to think since last *nacht*."

He stopped so suddenly that she nearly fell,

but he caught her close. "Martha, are you having second thoughts?"

She stretched to press her forehead against his. "*Nee*, Joel. You—you are someone I've wanted in my life—dreamed of more like . . . I can't even begin to explain."

He kissed her with gentle playfulness on the nose and she had to smile, but then he began their downward hike once more, carefully holding her arm.

Finally, he was able to lead her onto the solid macadam road. "I thought we could have a quick look inside the Ice Mine. You know they have the key over at the Sweden Haus."

"*Ach*," Martha murmured. "That would be a blessing to start us on our way, I think. You know the ice is just beginning to form."

"Yep." Joel took her arm and led her to the red-scalloped and green-trimmed cheer of the Sweden Haus. It was here, during the summer, that Gilbert Ellis, an *Englischer*, sold tickets to view the mine. He also ran a brisk trade at a gift shop adjacent to the rock walls of the mine. Gilbert was a *gut* friend to the Amish and also housed a few buggies and horses for them, should they want to do some shopping or run an errand to Coudersport.

Joel led Martha to the front porch overhang and knocked on the bright white wood. Mr. Ellis opened the door with a smile and a twist of his oversized mustache. His wife was right behind him with a tray of cookies, and Joel laughingly agreed to stop in for a few minutes.

"Our shoes are muddy," Martha pointed out.

"Oh, just give them a good wipe on the mat." Mrs. Ellis smiled. "There's so much water tracked in from the mine that it doesn't make a bit of difference."

They wiped their feet and followed the kind couple inside.

Joel leaned in close to Martha. "Will you talk a bit with Mrs. Ellis while I see about the key and a horse and buggy?"

She gave a demure nod. He caught the fresh scent of her hair and wanted to stop and make love to her right there on the planked wooden floor. He half shook his head and followed Mr. Ellis into the next room, thinking seriously that a woman like Martha Yoder would change his life forever.

Martha accepted a butter cookie with gratitude. She hadn't felt up to eating anything that morning, and the hike down had tired her some. She self-consciously adjusted the kerchief about her neck, then smiled as Mrs. Ellis set a tea tray between them, urging Martha to help herself. Then the older woman leaned back in a small rocking chair and smiled with kindness.

"You're courting, my dear?"

Martha's teacup rattled in its saucer, and she set it down on a nearby table. "Well," she began shyly. "We're to marry today in Coudersport."

Mrs. Ellis clapped her hands like a small child. "Then I must give you a gift."

Martha tried to protest, but her words were waved away. "Really, dear, it's my pleasure. Now just sit here a moment. I'll be right back."

Martha watched the trim lady's retreating back and took a moment to glance around her surroundings. It was odd how cheery but cluttered the room seemed, with all of its knickknacks and small mirrors. She was considering what it might be like to housekeep for Joel when Mrs. Ellis came bustling back. The older woman sat down and handed Martha a small black velvet box.

"Now, I know your people don't wear jewelry, but I would imagine you use garters to hold those woolen socks up?"

Martha nodded, feeling heat come into her cheeks, and then she opened the box. A frilly light blue garter rested inside. It was a beautiful, dainty thing and she fingered it gently.

"I wore that, on my thigh, on my wedding night," Mrs. Ellis confided in a near whisper.

"*Ach*, then it's very special. I—I cannot accept . . ."

"I have the memory, dear. I'd rather think of

111

it as making new memories . . . if you take my meaning."

Martha felt her blush deepen. "*Jah*, I understand." She closed the small box and slipped it into Joel's coat pocket, wondering excitedly what their wedding *nacht* would be like . . .

Joel slid the old-fashioned key into the lock of the green door that led to the Ice Mine. The mine itself had been discovered in the late eighteen hundreds, when a miner who had been seeking silver found a display of palatial summer ice instead. The clear and sparkling ice formed into huge icicles in the spring and summer but completely disappeared in the winter.

Joel opened the door, and a rush of cold air greeted them.

"Always refreshing and never the same, I think." He smiled down at Martha, who nodded in agreement; then he reached inside the darkness for the lantern and matches that were housed on the cave wall.

He turned up the light and held it aloft, carefully taking Martha's hand to lead her forward.

"Careful, now, the footing is slick."

He heard Martha's soft giggle. "Joel Umble, I know the bottom of this mine like I know my own woodpile, but still . . . it's wonderful to have someone care if I slip."

He half turned to her, letting the warm light of the lantern play over the delicate skin of her face. "You've always had to carry everyone, haven't you?"

She smiled and shook her head. "What else is there but to work for and love each other?"

"There's you—the wonderful, incredible you as a person and who you are in *Derr Herr*."

She pressed tight against him. "*Danki*, Joel Umble."

He kissed her in the haloed light, letting himself feel the chill of the air and the sweet warmth of her lips. Then he remembered where they were and the dangers of the Ice Mine shaft that plunged a *gut* forty feet into the earth. "Step over here, Martha. Do you want to hold the lantern? I'd like to touch the ice along the far wall."

There was a certain sanctity to the ice; a provision of *Gott*'s hand to cool the mind and body when it was needed most. Joel gave Martha the lantern and stepped to the first of several foot-thick ice formations. He felt happy as he placed his hand against the clear, wet surface, and then everything seemed to collapse before him. He knew he was having another vision, and even felt more in control of it, until he heard Martha's scream. He tried to move, to reach for her, but he couldn't break with the images that swallowed him. Her screams continued, and

113

then he saw her laboring to bring forth a child—her knees bent, her hair damp with sweat. He wanted to encourage her, to soothe her, but the scene shifted, and then he was walking in green grass.

There were seven tombstones, all alike in Amish style. He walked past them slowly, bending to touch the top of each one with his fingertips. He counted as he walked, each one a death knell ringing in his heart, and he heard Martha sobbing, her words blurred by tears, far away. He scrambled desperately in his mind to understand what she was saying, but the vision ended like a window closing, leaving him only with the cold of ice beneath his hand and within his pounding heart.

"Joel?" Martha's voice was clear in his ears.

He turned to face her.

"Joel, you're stone white. What's wrong? What did you see?"

"Nothing. It was . . . foolishness, that's all." *And yet every vision he'd seen had come true or been true . . . seven tombstones for seven children: his children, Martha's children.* He swallowed hard. *I will not put Martha through that; I'll change that vision and its outcome. I will not get her pregnant with my* kinner—*I don't care if I even have to marry her, then court her forever—there will be no deaths.*

Feeling both shaken and resolved, he ignored

her questioning expression and gently took the lantern back. He caught her cold fingers and blew out the light, leaving them standing still together in darkness before he shoved the door open with his shoulder and pulled her into the light.

# Chapter Fourteen

The sorrel horse, Trotter, made short work of the three-mile buggy trip to Coudersport. Still, Martha had time to study Joel's handsome profile as he sat with the reins easily held between his long thin fingers. He'd pushed his hat back a bit from his brow and she knew that he was deep in thought. He had experienced something at the Ice Mine, but she also knew that it was something he wanted to keep private . . . *After all, don't I have things about me that I want to keep close to my heart? Or am I to share every secret with Joel?*

She pushed aside the confusing thoughts as they rode into Coudersport. The small town was bustling with afternoon shoppers and shiny automobiles. There were also a few buggies and wagons, but Martha saw no other Amish, which relieved her in a way—she knew only too well of the Amish grapevine, even from community to community.

Although she had not been to the town in several years, Martha felt a renewed excitement just being able to look in the shop windows they passed. She was aware of Joel driving the buggy with confidence up the main street and knew a sudden pounding of her heart when they stopped at a rambling white house with bright green shutters. There was a white sign with black lettering on it, which she guessed read JUSTICE OF THE PEACE.

Joel confirmed her thoughts when he pulled Trotter to a stop, set the brake, then turned to smile at her. "Ready?"

"*Jah*," she said, looking him in the eyes.

Then he gestured to the sign with his chin. "Strange name, isn't it?"

Martha quickly agreed, having no idea what the name read. She found her voice after a tense moment. "We Amish have our odd names too."

"So we do." Joel jumped down, tied Trotter to the hitching post, then came around to Martha's side of the buggy. He reached up strong arms, and she couldn't help but delight in the firm press of his body as she slid to the ground.

As they walked hand in hand up the porch steps, it was impossible not to hear what sounded like a general ruckus coming from inside the *haus*, followed by the shrill squealing of a pig.

Joel looked at her and shrugged, then opened the screen door to knock hard, three times. If anything, the commotion from within seemed to escalate and the pig squeals became more persistent. After a second try at knocking, Joel grinned at her. "Do you think I dare open the door?"

"Why not?" she said smilingly in return. "At least we know somebody's home."

Joel knocked once more, then opened the door a crack. "Hello?"

Martha nearly lost her footing when Joel's shoulder bumped into her as something came barreling through the door from the other side. A huge pink pig with a mottled brown side ran out, squealing in ear-piercing bursts. This was followed by rapid footsteps and then voices from inside the *haus*.

Martha couldn't help but stifle a giggle when the pig gained the sidewalk and bowled over a gentleman in pointy-toed cowboy boots. The man raised his voice above the squeals.

"Dammit, Phillipe!"

But the pig kept on down the street.

An old man with a hook for one hand stepped out of the *haus*, pausing to nod to Martha and Joel. "Frank, don't you be yelling at my pig!"

"That's no pig, Pete Parker, and well you know it. He's a bona fide demon on four feet!" Frank, the man with the cowboy boots, pulled himself to his feet by way of the picket fence and hustled on down the street with a distinct limp.

"Sorry, folks, Frank's always held a grudge against Phillipe ever since the pig spooked his horse at the Memorial Day parade. So, what can I do you for? You'uns are Aim-ish, right?"

Martha heard Joel clear his throat. "Yes . . . we were hoping to see you, sir. About getting married."

Pete deftly scratched his gray head with his hooked hand. "Wal, now, that's a problem, seeing that the justice of the peace has run off."

"You mean you're not—" Joel began.

"Who, me? Nah. I'm Phillipe's proxy 'cause he don't speak much English. But he'll be back give or take an hour or two. We're havin' a shindig for the wife in one room and a birthday party for Pete Jr. in another. Hell, you two might as well come on in and join the fun!"

Martha watched as Joel nodded at the invitation and hugged the folds of his black coat more tightly about her, wondering *was en der weldt* kind of wedding they were to have . . .

One part of Joel's brain was occupied with the taste of frosted birthday cake, the radiant joy of young Pete Parker when he opened the gift of a BB gun from Phillipe, and avoiding the rather undisguised attempts of the young ladies across the hall at Mrs. Parker's tea to gain his attention. He knew, too, that Martha fairly steamed inside his coat at the sweet voices and understood that her jealousy was born of passion, which made his back warm and his shoulders tense.

The other part of his mind was trying desperately to think of how he'd explain to Martha that he didn't want to consummate their marriage yet . . . *Perhaps I can tell her that a longer courtship is what she deserves—what's proper—but then, she doesn't seem concerned with convention, and I wouldn't want her any way else . . .*

He edged closer to the spot where she stood stiffly, half in and half out of the tea party room. She'd removed her bonnet, and her delicate *kapp* looked a bit wilted.

"I wonder when that pig will be back?" he asked, bending to whisper in her shell-shaped ear.

She shrugged, then gave a little sniff. "I wouldn't think you'd care, with all of these *Englischers* trying to catch your eye."

"You're the only one who's caught my eye, Martha. I particularly like to remember holding you in my arms and—" *I am doing absolutely everything wrong if I'm planning not to fulfill our vows tonight . . .*

"And?" Her voice had softened, and he saw the simmering desire in her eyes. It was all he could do not to kiss her right there.

He was saved from a proper response by Pete Parker Sr. coming over and catching him by the arm. "Got somethin' I'd like to show ya, boy. Your fiancée can wait in here with the missus— Alice! 'Bout time your ladies' tea broke up, ain't it? The kids are goin' out to try that newfangled huly hoop thing, and this little gal could use some conversation."

Mrs. Parker took her husband's broad hint and

quickly hustled her friends out as they chattered and squealed amid the drifters from Pete Jr.'s party. She shut the door behind them all with a look of relief, and Joel's head rang in the sudden silence.

He gave a fleeting smile to Martha as the older man led him off down the hall, and Joel couldn't help but wonder what could possibly happen next in this strange *Englisch haus* . . .

"Have mercy, honey . . . I'm sorry I couldn't see to ya a bit sooner, but that tea group is like a herd of friendly bovines—always nudging and wanting more to eat!" Alice Parker gave Martha a wide smile.

Martha watched the small, plump woman move and gesture and decided she liked her.

"I'll just sweep away all of these plates and we'll have our own tea right now. I always keep some sandwiches and dainties out in the kitchen for later . . ."

"*Ach*, but you don't have to—" Martha began, ignoring the grumbling in her stomach.

"Why, it's your wedding day, isn't it? Let's do some celebrating." She gestured for Martha to come to the table and take a seat while she fluttered in and out of the wide swinging kitchen door. Martha watched with both hunger and delight as a multitude of crustless sandwiches and scones were soon spread out before her.

"Now, honey, we've got egg salad with those big olives and tuna and chicken salad and these are petit fours—a pain to make but a joy to eat! Oh, and let me help you out of that big coat. You must be hot."

Martha reluctantly let Mrs. Parker slide the coat from her shoulders, but then she felt naked somehow, longing for Joel and wondering how he was faring in the other room.

Joel was surprised at the number of maps Mr. Parker had displayed in what he called his "study." In truth, it was a congested closet of a room, but it still managed to present an interesting array of artifacts as well. And, beneath the single light bulb of the room, Mr. Parker seemed to change his demeanor from jovial proxy to serious older man.

"I don't believe it was a mistake that you came here today."

Joel glanced up in faint surprise from his study of a local map on a low wooden table. "You mean you think it's a *gut* thing Martha and I are getting married?"

Mr. Parker waved his hook hand, brushing aside Joel's question. "I want ta talk to you, boy. See, I don't just proxy for Phillipe . . . I'm not as silly as I might seem. But it keeps folks at a nice distance ta think that Pete Parker's lights are on but nobody's home . . ."

Joel straightened in fascination. "Why do you want to keep people away?"

The older man bent forward slightly. "I know a powerful secret, son . . . one told to me by another man with a hook for a hand."

Joel raised his eyebrows but kept listening.

"It was ol' Herb Cross. He lost his hand lumbering, but his mind was sharp up until the day he died. It was Herb that told me the secret. See, he had the second sight and—"

"What?"

Mr. Parker laughed, and his eyes narrowed a bit. "Deep calls to deep, so the Good Book says, and I know you've got the gift, same as Herb."

"I don't know what you're—"

"Ah, don't lie, son. It ain't healthy for the soul. I know you've got the gift but don't think of it as such. To you it's more of a curse, a fear of things past and things yet to come."

The image of the tombstones ran like a train through Joel's head, and he struggled to find words. "Wh—what do you want from me?"

"To add to your favor. To let you feel the weight of abundance."

"I'd rather not, thank you, sir," Joel said roughly. "I need to get back to Martha." He turned and would have stalked from the small room, but the hook barred his way.

"The secret, Joel Umble. You must give your word that you will carry it with you all your days until you find someone you know who will keep its sacred silence, and then they, too, shall pass it on."

Joel sighed. He had no true wish to know any secret, much less something that the other man held sacred, but he finally nodded.

Mr. Parker lowered his hook hand and gestured to the map that Joel had been studying a few minutes before. "Your Ice Mountain holds many secrets and mysteries of its own. But there is one place there that was sacred to a people who walked these woods long before us—the Lenni-Lenape. You know the name?"

"*Jah* . . . the Native Indians of this area." Joel was intrigued despite himself.

"Right, and the places where they buried their dead are large earthen mounds—made to look like small knolls or tiny hills. Made to blend in with the land and to keep curious outsiders away from the treasures of the mound and the sanctity of the dead. Still today, what you call archeologists search the land for these mounds and have found them in New York State and other places in Eastern Pennsylvania. But not here . . . and not on Ice Mountain either." The older man moved past Joel to indicate a spot on the map with the tip of his hook. "Do you know the spot, boy?"

Joel bent to study the map and recognized the marking of the creek on Ice Mountain and a heavily green area of dense woods. "That's up in the high timber. Nobody goes there much."

"There's a large burial mound in that area. You'll know it by the twin birches that mark either side. That's the secret, Joel . . . and you are bound to keep it until such time as you find someone else who will never tell, never seek to profit or gain by its history."

Joel looked up from the map. "How do you know that I am such a person?"

"Because I wouldn't have told you if you weren't." Mr. Parker blinked and clapped him on the back. Suddenly the "crazy" Pete Parker was back. "Think I hear Phillipe snorting this way. Time ta get ya hitched, *buwe*."

Joel nodded, staring at the odd man. "*Jah* . . . our marriage . . ."

# Chapter Fifteen

Martha stared down at the cream-colored paper of the registry. She bit her lip and glanced at the fast-drying black ink of Joel's cursive, hand-written name. She held the ink pen, feeling its odd weight like a stone on her heart. Then she straightened her spine and made a fast scribble ending with a dashing stroke. She slid the pen back in the holder and looked up at Joel.

"You have a beautiful signature, sweetheart," he murmured, then dropped a light kiss on her cheek. "And a new name."

Martha felt herself flush, pleased that *Derr Herr* had brought her through the obstacle—it might have been a small thing . . . *But then, I guess* Gott *cares for the little things in our lives too*.

"Well, you've both signed the registry, and Phillipe seems happy. Now y'all can go into the world as Mr. and Mrs. Umble." Pete Parker smiled at them while fondly rubbing the pig's ear.

Martha saw Mrs. Parker shed a tear, and then the other woman came forward to embrace her. Martha rejoiced in the press of the lady's small form, wishing her own mother might have been present.

She bade goodbye to the Parkers with genuine

feeling as they walked outside together, pausing to watch as Joel shook Mr. Parker's hand. The older couple had just gone back inside when Pete Jr. came running back carrying a handful of squirming earthworms.

The little boy had tears on his face and was making to bypass Martha when she put out a gentle hand to stop him. "What's the matter?"

"The other fellas were stompin' on them . . . I had to rescue them! I think I'll hide 'em in my room."

"Whoa, Pete," Joel said. "I don't think your *mamm* would appreciate that."

"*Nee*, she would not," Martha agreed. "But *kumme* here, and I'll show you a good home for them."

Martha watched from the corner of her eye as the child reluctantly followed her to the damp front flower bed of the house. She knelt down, heedless of her skirt on the messy ground, and began to dig at the earth with her bare hands . . .

Joel stood still for a long moment; he watched his wife's strong, slender hands in the dirt and swallowed hard. Martha had a genuineness of character that shook him to his soul . . . *How many brides would dig in the mud to help a crying child . . . ? A crying child . . .*

He had to shake himself and then hurried over to kneel beside Martha and the boy. The worms were soon thriving in the damp earth, and Pete Jr. gave Martha a grimy hug, then Joel helped her to her feet. The little boy was off down the street to some new adventure, and Joel looked down into Martha's gentle eyes and tenderly thumbed a streak of dirt from her dainty nose.

"You're wonderful, Martha Umble," he whispered. "Do you know that?"

She dropped her gaze and shook her head. "*Nee* . . . I just love the *kinner*." She flushed at her remark, and Joel struggled to put the image of the tombstones out of his mind . . . *The* kinner . . . *our children* . . .

He lowered his head and kissed her full lips long and sweet, careless of the fact that they stood on a main street for anyone to see. Then he came to himself and, holding her dirt-stained hand, helped her with care into the buggy.

He took out his pocket watch, easily handling the reins, then frowned slightly.

"What is it?" Martha asked.

"Our time is short for shopping."

He glanced over to see her smile. "Don't bother, Joel. I'm a plain woman . . ." She giggled. "I need no finery."

His frown deepened, despite her humor. "Well, I say that you do." He looked at her steadily. "Indulge me as your husband to gift you with a few things."

He eased the buggy past a shiny automobile,

then pulled Trotter up at a shop with bow-fronted windows. The writing on the glass read NANCY'S NICETIES, and he smiled in satisfaction. "Here we *geh*." He moved to lift her down, then grabbed her hand.

"*Ach*, Joel—I'm all dirty and—"

"Forget it. You're beautiful."

The hour may have been late in the afternoon, but Nancy of the niceties was all too willing to serve customers. Martha thought the *auld* woman resembled a fluttering good faerie as she came out from behind the counter to gauge sizes.

"You look like you're fresh from the garden and as pretty as a peach, child." Nancy briskly circled Martha's small waist with a tape measure. "I've got a very plain blue dress that might pass for Amish beneath your apron, if you'd like to try it on. And then we can get down to the important shopping . . ." Her voice trailed off suggestively, and Martha was confused when Nancy flashed her a cheery wink. "Maybe your nice young man here would care to take a walk around the block while we go to the back of the shop."

Joel seemed to take the hint and straightened with alacrity, but he paused to whisper against Martha's cheek. "You're all right? Get anything you want, Martha Umble, do you hear?" He pressed his leather wallet into her hands.

Martha nodded and then watched his retreating

back a bit wistfully. The store and Nancy seemed pleasant, but Martha was unused to such an array of dresses and finery. She felt overwhelmed but decided to enjoy herself for Joel's sake. But then Nancy flung open a dark blue curtain at the back of the shop, and Martha stopped still.

The small room was awash with lace and delicate batiste fabrics, as well as silks and satins. Two shapely mannequins wore a minimum of undergarments, and Martha felt herself blush. Her own underwear was limited to two ragged shifts, which she alternated for washing. She reached out tentative fingers to a short, peach-colored gown and Nancy smiled her approval.

"Just right for you and your pretty coloring."

"Thank you," Martha murmured, unused to such casual compliments. She considered the brevity of the gown and then decided with a soft sigh that Joel had seen her in far less . . .

Joel walked down the pleasant streets of the town without really paying much attention to where he was going. He was lost in thought after a long day of realizations and secrets . . . *And I still have my wedding* nacht *to get through without hurting Martha* . . . His footsteps slowed as he became aware of his surroundings and had the sudden feeling that he was being followed. He lowered the brim of his hat and took a quick glance over his shoulder. Three rough-looking *Englisch* men wearing plaid flannels were about twenty feet behind him. Joel turned down a shady side street, not wanting any trouble. He knew well enough that his people were sometimes not looked upon with favor. And now the men behind him began to snicker and call out. Joel exhaled slowly when he heard the insulting and guttural words.

"Clay ape, Aim-ish. Why don't you go back to the dirt where ya came from?"

Joel knew that the expression "clay ape" was not spoken idly. It was a cruel reference to his people's relationship with the soil but was also usually accompanied by rock throwing, or "clay-aping," as it was called. He had even heard of an Amish infant killed in his *mamm*'s arms when a vicious rock had found its mark. It wasn't that he was fearful; he knew both his back and arms were strong—yet the Amish were forbidden to use violence. He quickly decided, though, that it was his wedding day and he needed to get back to Martha.

The image of her sweet smile behind his eyes made him turn and face the other men. The first rock caught him unprepared and struck a glancing blow off his forehead. He saw illuminated dark-ness for a few seconds, lost his hat, then felt blood trail over his eye. Nonetheless, he raised unpracticed fists to his attackers and laid one of them low with a satisfying blow to the other man's chin. He felt a wave of dizziness that he ignored with determination, then turned a grim face to the other two. An axe handle stuck him solidly in the chest, seemingly out of nowhere, and he reeled backward, fully intending to continue the fight but suddenly unable to find his footing. Merciless blows seemed to rain down on him from every direction, and he felt himself slipping into darkness when a piercing whistle cut the air. He thought the sound funny somehow as it continued in sharp blasts. *Very funny . . . I'll have to tell Martha all about it . . .*

# Chapter Sixteen

"It weren't any of the townsfolk that did this, ma'am. Those men were from up north aways—troublemakers, and awful drunk too. I've got 'em locked up good 'n tight."

Martha heard the police chief's words but couldn't take her eyes from Joel where he lay in the big featherbed, oblivious to everything around him. She strained to listen as the old doctor murmured to himself while he tended her husband.

"Hmmm . . . bruised ribs . . . probable concussion . . . multiple contusions . . . but lucky to be alive." The doctor turned from Joel and snapped his black bag shut before looking at her. "I could send a nurse around to care for him tonight. He's likely to be delirious—might run a fever."

"*Nee*," Martha burst out, then lowered her voice. "I mean, no, thank you, Doctor. I will care for him as a wife should."

The old man studied her for a brief moment. "Good enough. I'll be around early tomorrow morning."

"*Jah* . . ." she whispered, moving forward to take the chair the doctor had abandoned close to the bed. She vaguely heard the two men mutter to each other as they left the honeymoon suite of the inn.

"That's one helluva wedding night . . ."

"Shush! She'll hear . . ."

The door closed gently, and she was finally alone to be with Joel. The police had found her in Nancy's store, and she had followed them shakily down the street to the Buttonwood Inn, where Joel had been brought to be seen by the doctor. Now he lay without his shirt or suspenders, the crisp white sheets drawn up to his waist. She might have thought he was merely sleeping if it weren't for the bruises that marked him in the glare of the bedside electric lamp. And there was also the bandage wrapped round his head, stark white against the rumpled darkness of his hair.

She prayed softly, feeling tears flood her eyes as she wished there was something more she might do. But then Joel stirred, and she leaned closer, gently letting her fingers hover over his right hand. He groaned faintly, and she nearly jumped at the raw sound.

"Joel, shhh . . . it's all right."

"*Nee*," he breathed, flinging an arm across his eyes. "Not right . . . How can I tell her? . . . Seven times . . . Seven stones . . . Keep the secret . . . Keep her whole . . ." His voice trailed off in a child's singsong rhyme, and then he was still again.

Martha bathed his face and chest with cool

134

water from a nearby bowl and pitcher and kept fierce watch over him. At one point, he reared up and caught her shoulders in a painful grip. "Don't hurt her! Must not hurt her . . . Keep to the courtship . . . Go on courting . . ."

She eased him back against the pillows when his grip slackened and slowly turned his fevered words over in her mind . . .

Joel came awake in painful degrees. His head throbbed, and it hurt to take a breath. But at the first thought of Martha, he risked opening his eyes.

"With us again, son?"

Joel blinked, and even that hurt. He didn't recognize the aged voice or the walrus mustache on the round face peering down into his own, but he nodded.

"Good. Your wife tells me you were out of it most of the night, but you'll pull through."

"Martha?" His voice rasped in his own ears.

"She's right here. I'll leave you a bit of something for the pain, and you should be yourself after a week or so."

*A week . . . a week . . .* He cudgeled his brain for the reason that the time seemed impossibly long, and then realization dawned. *I missed our wedding* nacht . . . Another thought struck and he almost sat up. *We've got to get back to Ice Mountain today . . .*

He heard the door close; then Martha sat down next to him. "That was Dr. McGuire. He saw you last evening. *Ach*, how do you feel, Joel?"

He half smiled. "Wretched, but well enough for us to *geh* back home today."

"*Nee*," she said firmly.

"Martha—we're up against a ticking clock here—your family, my mother, not to mention Judah. I wanted to announce our marriage in church service today."

"The owners of the inn here, the *Englisch* Summerson family, have asked us to stay free of charge. They feel so bad that this happened in their town."

Joel blew out a breath of frustration and gingerly put a hand to his side; then he sat up with a gasp of pain that he tried to suppress for Martha's sake.

Martha pushed him back, seemingly without compunction, and his jaw tightened. "Martha Umble . . . I am your husband, and you must obey—"

She broke out in a casual burst of laughter. "Obey you? I think not—not when you're hurting so."

He frowned at her, not knowing exactly how to deal with her strong will and her obvious concern for him. He wanted to level the field with her, and a small idea began to form at the back of his throbbing head.

"We had no wedding *nacht* . . . I regret that," he said softly. *Not that I would have done anything after that vision . . . Maybe the knock on my head will do me* gut *and I'll be free of this miserable second sight . . .*

He came back to the moment and saw Martha eyeing him carefully, cautiously, and he managed to suppress a grin.

"I, too, regret it, Joel," she whispered.

Against his will, his body responded to the cadence of her soft words, and he felt himself becoming confused as to what he was trying to accomplish . . . *Level the field . . . Right . . .*

"Take your hair down," he said abruptly, and was glad when her doe eyes widened a fraction.

Instead of obeying his command, though, she leaned forward and pressed a gentle hand to his bandaged forehead. "Perhaps you have a fever . . . I will give you some of the medicine the doctor left." She turned away, and he moved restlessly in the big bed.

"I don't want the medicine. *Danki.*"

She raised a perfectly arched brow at him and poured something from a brown vial into a small glass of water. "You may not want it, Joel, but you'll have it all the same. You forget that I am used to the occasional tempers of those who are in pain."

Her pretty mouth turned down tiredly for a

moment, and he felt like an ass. *Here she is . . . caring for me, always caring for someone, and I'm behaving like a five-year-old . . .*

He drank the contents of the glass she held to his lips without protest, and in a few minutes, his pain seemed to drift pleasantly away. He relaxed into the thick mattress and eyed Martha with pleasure. "Please, *sei se gut*, take your hair down, my wife." He felt the words slip easily from his mouth, and his mind filled with lulling, arousing images of her naked in his arms.

He heard her brief sigh of consent, and he followed her movements when she rose to cross the room and turn the lock on the door. She turned back to face him as he lay waiting and he saw her reach for the pins that held the luscious fall of her hair in place . . .

Martha watched his eyes close, the thick dark lashes lying in even crescents against his bruised and flushed cheeks, and she dropped her hands from her hair with a faint smile. *He needs to rest, and I must not worry about my family at home . . . I know* Derr Herr *will bless and keep them—keep them safe from Judah . . .*

*He was hot, burning with need. Sensation trailed down his back in molten pinpricks, leaving him in a state of near-painful arousal. Martha seemed both close and far away, evading his hands and*

138

*the lift of his hips. He wanted her so badly that his mouth watered, and then she was tangled in the sheets next to him. He forgot about his injuries; they seemed as nothing compared to his desire. He found the tight peaks of her breasts with his hands, and his mouth met hers until everything convulsed in a heated rush of passion that left him gasping for breath . . .*

Joel awoke with a start, sucking in air and realizing that it had merely been a dream . . . He shivered and glanced around, wanting Martha. He half turned and saw her sleeping soundly atop the covers, fully dressed. Faint, bruise-like circles were beneath her eyes, and he knew she must be exhausted. Yet even in sleep, she held herself stiff, obviously afraid that she'd hurt him in some way by getting too close. The only concession to comfort she'd made had been to remove the kerchief from about her neck, and he winced as the sunlight played on the marks still visible on her pale throat. Joel lay back down and put out a tentative hand to press against her abdomen, feeling her breathe. He closed his eyes, able to forget his worries for a while, as the even softness of Martha's breath lulled him back to dreams . . .

# Chapter Seventeen

"Do you want me to manage the reins, Joel?" Martha asked the question for what seemed like the fifth time and was frustrated once more by the shake of his dark head, now absent its white bandage.

"I'm fine, Martha. Don't worry."

She sighed to herself and glanced down at Trotter's broad rump as the horse quickly ate up the distance to Ice Mountain. She had persuaded Joel to rest for a full day, but then he'd insisted on rising, eaten a hearty breakfast, and kissed her into agreeing that they should *geh* home.

An hour slipped by, and soon the wild ferns that were unique to Ice Mountain began to appear. Tiny buds of forsythia dotted pale brown branches, and the pines seemed to take heart and stand taller, shaking off winter's burden. The lichen, the rock, and the bright green mosses all stood out in royal greeting to Martha's heart as she realized that it was spring.

"Pretty, isn't it?" Joel asked, and she nodded. He whistled softly. "But not half as pretty as you, Martha Umble."

She knew her cheeks flamed in a blush, but she smiled at him all the same. Here was her husband—the one of her heart's desire and dreams! And *Gott* had made it possible that they should wed.

Martha waited as Joel paid Mr. Ellis for Trotter's time and the buggy, and she was glad when the kind *Englisch* man offered her husband a stout walking stick.

The hike up the mountain was a good mile or so, and she watched him out of the corner of her eye, trying to make sure that he was not exerting himself overmuch. There had been no mention of stopping at the Ice Mine—even for a few minutes. Whatever he had seen there, he didn't want to share, and Martha shied away from raising the issue.

The smell of the clean, fragrant mountain air was invigorating to the senses, and Martha rejoiced inside when they cleared the tree line at the head of the trail.

"I'm anxious to see how my family fared," Martha said softly as they walked over the pine needle–laden floor of the woods leading to the community.

He squeezed her hand comfortingly. "May is very capable; no harm will have come to them."

Martha nodded, trying not to wonder about May's capabilities and telling herself sternly that Joel had married her and not the young healer of the mountain.

Then she realized that the small path they were on would lead directly past Sol Kauffman's store—an easy spot for one and all to learn word that she and Joel were together. "We're going past the store?"

"You betcha, sweetheart." Joel gave her a quick smile. "There's no better place to get the word around about us. We'll stop by Sol's, and then we'll swing past my *mamm*'s to break the news, and then I'll see you home to your folks . . . our folks. Is that all right?"

A thousand thoughts suddenly spilled in a tumult through her mind. "Joel?" She wet her lips and plunged into the chaos of her thinking. "We're to live at your *haus*? What about Judah? And your *mamm*, what will she say? How can she welcome three invalids into her home? And . . ."

He stopped and leaned over to press his forehead against hers. "Martha," he whispered. "It's going to be *gut* . . . or, at the very least, interesting." He smiled and kissed the tip of her nose. "And have no more fear of Judah. I will deal with him."

"But how . . . ?"

She would have gone on, but he grabbed her hand again and marched her purposefully forward.

Joel felt there was something different going on in the community as soon as they neared the store. Then he saw the groups of concerned-looking men and women—the men talking fast

142

while the bonneted women doled out soup and cut sandwiches. Tim Fisher, a cabinetmaker, caught sight of Joel and motioned him forward. "Here's Joel Umble . . . perhaps he's seen the *buwe*."

Joel squeezed Martha's hand tightly. "What *buwe*?"

"Young Jared Mast is missing . . . has been for nearly two days."

Joel had a brief image of the little boy who'd caught Martha and himself kissing before they'd left the mountain to marry . . . "Where was he last seen?"

"Near the creek . . ." Tim's voice lowered. "We've searched downstream."

Joel nodded, then bent to whisper to Martha. "Dan Zook's murderer is still loose somewhere. I've got to try to find Jared."

He wasn't surprised when Martha looked up at him with solemn eyes. "I know this mountain well, Joel Umble, and I am fast and fleet as a deer. I must search too."

He nodded, once more entranced by her sense of purpose and strength. And he knew her to be right about her abilities and knowledge of the mountain. Then a thought struck him—Judah might track the child with his trapping skills— but he had no desire to ask for his *bruder*'s whereabouts and wasn't even sure that Judah would help if he could . . .

• • •

Martha wanted more than anything to see her family and to tell them all about her wedding day, but she could not bear to think of little Jared Mast alone in the woods. She ran, searching all of the childish haunts that she could remember from her own youth, and then turned toward the swamp. Her shoes began to make sucking sounds in the damp, dark earth, and she prayed, even as she searched, that the child would not have found himself near the place. She rounded a stand of tamarack pines, then came to a dragging halt. Judah crouched before her, intent on skinning something on the ground, but he looked up with a leer when he caught sight of her.

"There is a child lost, Judah . . . little Jared Mast. I am searching for him."

She knew she could not outrun him, and she wet her lips, determined to at least keep a distance between them. She saw his eyes *geh* to the kerchief about her neck and lifted her chin. "I've heard word of the missing brat, but also had traps in this area." He gestured toward the bloody ground, then wiped his wet hands on his pants. "You seem to be a little worse for wear since our last bundling . . ."

"Do you mean since you tried to choke me to death?"

She was surprised to see his face flush. "I—I

144

meant to choke the witchery from you, Martha. Not to take your life."

"Then I suppose it is a relief to find yourself not a murderer." She kept her voice even. "But I will not stand here and speak of these things when Jared might be in bad trouble." She wondered briefly if Judah would actually let her *geh* . . . *He seems strangely unbalanced, almost as if he truly did not want to take my life. I wonder if I might gain his sympathy and lead him back to Sol's store . . .*

But even as she pondered the issue, he quickly closed the distance between them and laid a bloody hand on the blue sleeve of her dress. She closed her eyes and willed herself not to scream. She knew it would only excite him more.

Joel was staring at the map of the mountain, noting which places had already been searched, when Sol Kauffman moved next to him and spoke low. "Temperatures drop at night . . . it doesn't look *gut*."

Joel shook his head. "*Derr Herr* knows where the child is."

"*Jah* . . . that be true enough. More than likely the *buwe* had some secret hiding place and—"

"Wait," Joel snapped. "What did you say?"

"I said that the child must have some place secret he goes."

*That's it . . . someplace secret . . .* Joel turned with the heavy walking staff in his hands. "I'll *geh* to the high timber and search."

Sol waved a hamlike hand in front of Joel's face. "Men have already searched there, yesterday."

Joel moved past the older man. "Still, it never hurts to have a second pair of eyes *geh* over things." He ignored the pain in his ribs and Sol's bemused expression, then hurried on to climb further up the mountainside.

Joel had to stop and catch harsh breaths more than once as he headed for the high timber. He thought long and hard as he moved, going over in his mind the map that Pete Parker had shown him. If nothing else, perhaps the simple vantage point of the Indian burial mound might offer him some perspective.

His mind drifted to Martha, and he wondered at the fact that she was now his wife. *My wife . . . to hold and protect, though little* gut *I did her last* nacht *. . . I could barely protect myself the other day . . .*

He looked up and saw large twin birch trees standing on either side of what looked like a simple hill, with mud and new grass showing through. And then he saw it . . . a small black Amish hat at the base of the mound. He hurried forward and grasped the child's hat, then looked up in surprise as a tall *Englisch* man walked around the mound, carrying Jared Mast in his thick arms.

"Is this little man the one you seek?"

Joel nodded, stepping nearer to see that Jared's eyes were open but that he had a thick bump on his pale forehead and cuts and scratches on his small face and arms.

"Where did you find him?"

"Oh, the weather was so nice today that I decided to do some fishing. He was down the bank aways, near the head of the creek."

"Well, I've got to thank you, and I'm sure Jared's family would want to . . . Can you follow me back to the community with him?" Joel asked.

"I'd actually be more than happy to. You see, I've been staying over at one of the cabins beyond the ridge, but I really need a job to pick up some pocket money. Do you know of anyone who might need a hired hand?"

Joel smiled and put out his right hand. "I'm Joel Umble, and I'd surely be glad of another man about the place. My best friend—well, he had to move . . . So, anyway, if you can do a little farming or know anything about sheep . . ."

The tall man's blue eyes twinkled as he neatly held Jared and returned Joel's handshake. "Sebastian."

Joel waited for a surname, but none seemed forthcoming, and that was all right with him. They began to walk together down the mountain, but Sebastian veered off on a side path that Joel would not have taken. "The main trail is faster," Joel commented.

"It is important that you take this path, Joel Umble." Sebastian gave him a wide smile, and Joel shrugged.

"Lead on, then."

Joel said the words lightly, but something triggered in his heart as he edged down the mountain after the tall man bearing the child. *Did I just give permission for something more than a different path?* He shook himself with a half smile. *I'm overtired . . .*

Martha's first impulse was to blurt out to Judah the fact that she and Joel were married. But as his hand tightened on her arm, she instinctively knew that such news might not be in her best interest. "Judah, let *geh*. You're hurting me."

She saw his eyes glitter and hid a groan. *Never tell him I'm in pain . . . never . . .*

"Judah. I'm going back to Sol Kauffman's. Do you—do you want to *kumme* and help me look for Jared?" She saw the confusion in his eyes at her gentle tone, but then he jerked her close. "You would use soft words to hex me."

"She is no hex!"

Martha cried out in relief as Joel's voice echoed in the clearing. She saw him and a large man carrying an alert Jared Mast, and she pulled from

Judah to cross the brief space into her husband's arms.

"Joel," Judah sneered. "What game do you play at now? What is this *maedel* to you?"

Martha felt Joel's arms about her and took a deep breath, anticipating the harsh words to come from Judah, despite the *Englischer*'s presence.

"Judah, you would curse Martha—the one who is now my wife and your sister. Stop this *narrish* behavior and accept what you cannot change."

Martha saw the look of disbelief on Judah's face, but Joel was already shepherding her to turn away. She jumped when she heard Judah's enraged snarl.

"This is not over, Joel Umble! We will have this out, and in the end, she will be mine."

Martha paused as Joel spoke over his shoulder in even tones. "*Jah*, my *bruder*, we will have this out, I assure you."

Then Joel led her on up the path. "Martha, meet Sebastian—er, Sebastian—he found Jared."

Martha smiled in greeting, thankful the child was well. But she could not help but feel as though Judah stared after them with menacing eyes . . .

# Chapter Eighteen

"That went well, don't you think?" Joel's voice was teasing and merry, and his spirits lifted when he saw that Martha couldn't resist smiling.

They'd *kumme* into the sheep barn for a brief respite after telling Joel's *mamm* of their marriage. Sarah Umble was still sobbing into Puddles' sleek fur when Joel walked with Martha outdoors.

"Your *mamm* doesn't favor me, to say the least," Martha said, bending to pet the woolly back of a sheep in the pen.

"She's very anxious about change, about life, about everything." He drew up close to Martha and eased in front of the wooden slats of the pen. "Don't worry. And why don't you try giving me a pet?"

He watched her smile up at him in the sunlight that filtered through the thin cracks in the barn. She was dark and light, a gift from *Derr Herr*, and he wanted so badly to keep her safe. *Even from myself . . . But maybe just a touch, a kiss . . . small things for a husband to ask . . .* Yet he was unprepared for the raw passion she gave when his mouth found hers. She laced her slender arms about his neck and met his tongue with tiny, definitive strokes of her own. He forgot everything as she pressed full-length against him; the peaks of her breasts were hard against his chest and he groaned aloud when she slipped one hand down to skim his waist. His eyes widened in pleasurable shock, and he turned her so that her back was against the wooden wall of the barn.

*Right here . . . right now . . .* His body demanded what his mind could not. He remembered the tombstones and wrenched himself away from her with a hoarse cry.

He glanced at her and saw the bereft expression on her pretty face. "Joel—I—did I? I'm sorry . . ."

"*Nee*, sweetheart," he finally managed between breaths. He swallowed hard. "I want to court you for a time, woo you, win you . . . Will you let me do that? A courtship here, in the presence of all, on Ice Mountain . . ."

He saw the tears tremble on her lashes and wanted to kick himself.

"Then we will not be as man and wife? Not share the same bed?"

He thought fast, ignoring the subliminal roar that screamed he could not possibly share a bed with her . . . "We will sleep together, of course." He reached to stroke her cheek. "I—I just want to give you some time . . ."

He felt more than saw her nod hesitantly, and his gut twisted at the pain he knew he was causing her . . . But better a small pain now than that of death and loss . . . *I will never get her with child—never.* He took her small, work-calloused hand into his very carefully. "*Kumme*, my *frau*, let us *geh* and see your folks." He forced himself to ignore her trembling as they left the dimness of the barn for the bright sunlight of day.

Two days later, Martha had to shake herself in the middle of her famiiy's move to Joel's *haus* to try and forget his words in the barn. *A courtship . . . even though we are married . . . even though I want no part of more time to court . . .* But then she remembered Joel's mutterings while he'd been injured on their wedding *nacht . . . He'd talked in his delirium about lengthening the courtship at that time. Could it be that even then he regretted that he married me?* She was trying to push such thoughts aside when her *grossmuder* must have noticed her standing idle and called to her.

"Well, girlie. This is a change of the order of things, don't you think? Or are ya just day-dreaming about your man?"

Martha felt herself flush and went to sit on the small chair near her grandmother's bed. "I'm thinking, Grossmuder, that's all. The last two days have been—difficult."

Esther Yoder chuckled faintly. "I'd like to have been there to see Eli Loftus when he heard of yer wedding."

Martha suppressed a shudder. "*Nee.* I'm glad you missed that."

Martha's mind drifted back to the day before, when she and Joel had gone to the bishop's home to reveal their marriage.

"We realize," Joel had said, "this is not the traditional way of our people, but we all know of those who have been married in the *Englisch* world and then have been accepted as truly wed by the bishop and church community."

"It is not merely a formality that makes a marriage, *buwe*. And how foolhardy you've been to take a hex such as this to your heart. What did your older *bruder* counsel?"

Martha had told Joel some of the things Judah had claimed the bishop had said about her, and she knew her husband was not going to be distracted by wily questions or speaking. Still, she could tell from the tenseness of his body that Joel was angry. And she'd listened to the subtle tones of her husband's voice and knew he would not stand for much more.

"Judah, to say the very least, was not taken into our counsel, nor was he aware that we had plans to marry. And I fear, Bishop Loftus, we will have to leave if you plan on continuing to insult my wife."

Martha probably would have laughed, had she been able to, as the bishop gobbled like a spring turkey. He gritted his teeth and opened his mouth, only to be halted by Judah's abrupt entrance. Martha thought it odd that Judah felt confident enough in the place not to knock, but this thought drifted quickly away as Joel began to speak.

"Judah. It's *gut* that you are here. I want to introduce you more formally to my wife, Martha Umble. I will begin the movement of her family to our home as soon as possible."

Judah took a step nearer to Joel, and Martha had wanted to cringe at the fury in the other man's eyes.

"I—I am the first *sohn*! The eldest! And I will not permit this—this hex and her coven to move to Mamm's home." Judah's face grew red, but then the bishop spoke in an almost hypnotic tone.

"Never mind, Judah. No marriage based on evil will last, and time will bear that out. We must wait and see the fullness of loss that your younger *bruder* will reap by sowing on unholy ground. Therefore I will invite you to come and make your home here with me, the better for your training in the Ordnung and your certain future as both a church and community leader."

Martha had shivered at the hateful words, but then she looked to Judah and saw an almost peaceful calm replace the anger on his face. It was as if he was lulled by the bishop's eerie words, and she had wondered at the evil in both men . . .

"Now you, Grossmuder . . ." Joel brought Martha

back to the present by swiping a kiss on her cheek. She watched him gently wrap her grandmother in the many quilts he had brought to the *haus*. She automatically moved to help, but wondered whether his light kiss had been real or merely a ruse to make her family think he loved her . . . *Love me . . . I've never thought of it . . . I just focused on the marriage and having Joel in my life forever . . . But does he love me?* It was a question meant for another time. Right now, she was forced to focus on the move . . .

Joel concentrated on his footsteps carefully as he carried fragile Esther Yoder down to his home. At the very least, he was happy that his *mamm* seemed to accept the facts of his marriage and the coming of the Yoders. Although she had sobbed for nearly an hour when Judah had *kumme* and taken away his possessions. *Yes, Judah is living and training under an evil man . . . What can I do to help my* bruder? *And do I really want to help him?* He rallied his focus as the newly hired *Englisch* hand, Sebastian, passed him carrying a barrel holding the Yoders' scant possessions.

"You bear a beautiful burden—if it be a burden, Joel?"

Joel had to smile down at his new *grossmuder* at the merry words. "*Jah*, truly beautiful."

He wanted to say the same thing to Martha as he saw her in the distance climbing the steps to his home. They'd had little time to talk or even to see each other with the sudden move; now he wanted to seek her out.

He reached the boundaries of his family's farm and soon gained the steps with the spritely Esther Yoder held safe in his arms. And then he took her to the aired and ready guest room. He knew that they still needed to figure out the living arrangement of the rooms but felt that his new *grossmuder* would blossom with the sunlit windows at the back of the house.

"Go on now, *sohn*." She reached to pat his cheek when he'd placed her on the bed. "*Geh* and see your wife for a minute or two."

"How do you know what I'm thinking?" he asked with a smile.

"*Ach*," she said softly, her face softening in memory. "I was once young and married too."

He bent and kissed her gently on her rose petal–soft cheek, then left the room, leaving the door ajar so that she might feel part of the bustling atmosphere of the *haus*.

He found the staircase unoccupied for a moment and went upstairs to look for Martha. He found her in his and Judah's *auld* room. She was standing facing the window, looking outside, but she turned when he came into the room and eased the door closed.

"Martha?"

"*Ach*, Joel—I don't mean to be idle, but the sheep look so lovely against the new grass."

He crossed the room and put an iron grip on his desire to touch her . . . *I'll use my words to touch her instead* . . . The thought came unbidden and fast, and he gazed down at the bed he'd occupied for so long.

"You find beauty in uncommon things," he said huskily.

She smiled her beautiful smile, and he shoved his hands into the pockets of his black wool pants. "And you know how to flatter, I think," she replied.

His gaze slipped from her profile to the high, rounded curves of her breasts beneath her dress and apron and he swallowed hard. "It's not flattery to compliment your wife."

He didn't miss the sudden downturning of her mouth and knew what she was thinking . . . *Not a wife. Not in truth* . . . He took a step closer. He could smell the fresh scent of her hair and something sweet and womanly that he knew to be uniquely Martha. *Dear* Gott . . . *there's a bed right here* . . . But she deserved so much more than to be taken on a single bed in the room he'd shared with Judah . . . *And I'm not taking . . . I'm courting . . .*

"Will you bundle with me tonight?" she asked softly, wistfully. "That is part of courting."

"*Jah*," he whispered. "It is, and I will." *Even though it's going to kill me not to touch you . . .*

# Chapter Nineteen

Later that evening, Martha had a free moment to bend and pet the sleek cat, Puddles, who seemed to make himself at home anywhere. Now the cat was curled up on a kitchen chair where Martha had thought to sit to drink a cup of tea.

She looked up from the animal as Joel and his *mamm* came in through the back door.

"There he is," Sarah Umble cried as she scooped Puddles up into her arms and held him very close while rocking slightly.

Martha rose to her feet and glanced from mother to *sohn*. "I—uh—I do not want to intrude on your time together. I was going to make tea . . . Perhaps I can make some for you both before I bid my family *gut nacht*."

"*Nee*, Martha. Sit down and I'll make the tea for you and Mamm," Joel said with a flash of his blue eyes. "You are no servant or caregiver, here to fetch and carry."

"And I have been no servant, Joel," Martha contradicted softly. "It was my privilege and pleasure to care for my family."

She heard his sigh. "I know, Martha. I just want things to be easier for you now."

Joel's mother looked up at her, being shorter by at least a few inches. "He said he'll make tea. He'll make tea. Now sit!"

Martha dropped hastily into the chair and waited, having no desire to upset her new mother-in-law.

Joel sighed again. "Mamm . . ."

"I'll say what I like. It was my *haus* . . . maybe it still is. Is it?" She lowered pleading eyes to Martha's.

"Of course it's your home." Martha ignored the impulse to hug the older woman. "Joel and I will perhaps build something in the coming year and you will be free of all of these new people."

Martha met Joel's eyes, hoping she'd said the right thing, and was relieved when he nodded slightly, then turned to the sink.

Sarah Umble slid onto a bench at the table, and Martha smiled at her. Joel's *mamm* looked down at the cat in her lap, then back up to eye Martha suspiciously.

"Are you pregnant?"

Martha burst out laughing, while Joel dropped a teacup into the sink.

"Mamm!"

"What? I can ask. No harm in asking."

Martha reached across the table to pat Sarah's hand and quickly swallowed her laughter. "*Nee*, I'm not pregnant . . ." *And nor am I likely to be any time soon . . .*

* * *

Joel was exhausted—not only because of the pain in his still-healing ribs but also because he hadn't been sleeping well and now faced the prospect of bundling with Martha in the large wood-hewn bed of the master bedroom. As was the custom of his people, his *mamm* had moved her things to one of the smaller bedrooms upstairs, while he and Martha took over the large room on the main floor. He opened the door, then automatically pulled it shut behind him while he stared at Martha.

She had the top of her shift ruched down around her hips and was washing her arms and breasts with a cloth and water from the bowl and pitcher. She glanced up at him and stood frozen, her full lips forming a single "O" of surprise.

"I—I can *geh* out," he choked, never wanting to do something less in his life. His eyes helplessly followed the rivulets of water down the supple white curves of her body. A single lantern burned on the dresser, and her full breasts glowed gold.

"*Nee*. I'm sorry, Joel. I can hurry." She wriggled her hips, and her shift fell to the hardwood floor, leaving her completely naked to his hungry gaze. She sloshed the cloth against her belly and dipped the fabric back into the bowl.

"Wait," he said softly.

She looked at him, and he was across the floor in three steps, his feet coming to land at her side.

He put his much larger hand over her slender fingers and pushed to submerge the cloth deep into the water.

"Will you allow me to finish for you?" he asked, his eyes touching her everywhere.

"*Jah,*" she whispered.

He tugged the cloth free of her fingers, and she moved her hands to her sides, giving him complete freedom, he knew, to touch her anywhere he wanted . . .

Martha couldn't help the delighted shiver that trailed down her back when Joel stepped behind her and bent to put his mouth at the juncture of her neck and shoulder. He kissed her with tiny, sucking motions, loosening her hair; and all while he trailed warm water down her throat and breasts. Her nipples stung with sensation as she felt his fingers tighten on the cloth. She was conscious of her body more so now beneath his touch than at any other time in her life. She straightened her shoulders and arched her back, and he groaned aloud as their bodies touched.

He dropped the cloth, and she turned by instinct within the circle of his arms. She stood on tiptoe and found his mouth, pressing her wet body to his fully clothed frame.

"Dear *Gott*, Martha . . ." He kissed her in return, sliding his hands to her waist, then hips. He pulled her tight against him, and she felt the hard press of his body, burning like a brand against her belly.

It all seemed so wonderfully natural, and her heart pounded in her chest as she thought of the bed so near. But Joel dropped to his knees before her, and she put a hand down to touch his dark hair, trying to steady herself against the onslaught of his hot mouth. He kissed her everywhere, leaving her gasping with desire. She swallowed wanton cries from the back of her throat, then clung to the shoulders of his damp shirt.

"Joel—please. *Sei se gut . . .*" She both knew and didn't know what it was she wanted, only that she had to press her thighs together in hopes of quelling the startling flame that burned within her.

Joel got to his feet and swung her up in his arms, carrying her to the freshly made bed. He laid her down, then leaned over her with arms that trembled as she arched toward him in supplication and hot want. But he pulled away abruptly with a hoarse cry and walked out of the room in long strides, leaving Martha to turn into the feather pillow and sob.

Joel's breath came in harsh gasps as he practically ran from the *haus* to the relative privacy of the sheep barn. His body felt as though it burned beneath his clothing, and he turned against the far back wall, leaning his head on his forearm and using his other hand to find the hardness that throbbed against his belly. He sought release in frantic motions, then sank into the hay on his knees when it was over. His breathing still roared in his ears as he thought of Martha, wanting her so badly that he could taste it, but then he remembered the vision, and his body cooled rapidly . . .

Martha saw the hectic color in his fine-boned cheeks when he came back into their room. She'd given up on crying and instead had drawn a quilt from a nearby chest. She rolled the quilt until it was firm, then carefully laid it down the center of the bed. She did not know where there was a bundling board, so the quilt would have to do.

"Do you want me to turn the light down while I undress?" he asked in a husky voice.

Martha shook her head and turned her back to him as she curled into a small ball on her side of the rolled quilt. She heard the subtle slide of fabric being removed and then the few patters of straight pins being placed on the dresser. She heard the brisk splash of water from the basin, and then he was climbing into bed next to her.

She felt that he was looking at her, but squeezed her eyes shut tightly, feigning sleep.

"Martha?" he whispered. "Can we talk?"

She didn't answer, and when he finally extinguished the lamp, she heard him sigh softly as he lay down in the darkness.

# Chapter Twenty

Joel's days spun into increasingly frantic motion as the spring lambing came early and suddenly to the farm. Lost Lenore was first, and she labored long while Joel waited. Finally, he knew he'd have to help her. It was nearly four a.m., and he looked in on Martha sleeping next to the bundled quilt, wishing he could feel her warmth. Instead, he pulled the pins from his shirt rather carelessly and took it off. Lambing could be a cold, messy business, but it was well worth it in the end.

He went out to the sheep pen where Lenore had been isolated, as all laboring ewes were. Then he scrubbed up from the bucket of hot, soapy water he'd brought from the *haus* and used a disinfectant on his hands. He was gentle, careful not to hurt the sheep, but her uterus was a tangled mass of legs and heads. Joel closed his eyes and imagined the layout of each twin lamb's body. He straightened a bent foreleg, which seemed to be the holdup, and the first lamb was shortly delivered. He rubbed it in the hay quickly, then turned back to Lenore. Twins were a common but sometimes dangerous outcome for a ewe, and if he wasn't fast enough, the second lamb could stop breathing or be rejected by the mother. He hurried with the next birth, seeing that this lamb was covered in amniotic fluid and not breathing. Joel grabbed a towel and started to rub with frantic motions.

"*Kumme* on," he muttered. "*Kumme* on."

"Turn her over."

Joel's head snapped up with a start. Sebastian, the hired *Englisch* man, stood with a boot on the pen's wooden rail.

Joel looked back down at the lamb and turned it over onto its back, figuring he had nothing to lose. Immediately the lamb snorted and struggled to get free. Joel smiled and gave it the same hay treatment as its twin, then breathed a long sigh of relief when Lenore swung around to examine both lambs with interest.

Joel sank back on his knees and looked over to Sebastian. "Thanks for the tip."

The other man tossed him a towel. "Not a problem, Joel."

"What are you doing up at this hour? I wish I had a better place for you to sleep than the big barn, but the *haus* is pretty well full up."

Sebastian laughed. "It's a fair amount of comfort that you've given me, and all the privacy I could want. And it's much better than hiking to the cabins on the other side of the mountain every day."

Joel nodded, wiping himself down. He turned to watch with satisfaction as the lambs tried to rise and suckle. "Always the best part."

"You're a true shepherd, Joel, right down to your soul."

"*Danki . . .*" Joel eased himself to his feet. "But sometimes I wonder . . ."

"About?"

"*Ach* . . . about leading a family—or—Martha's family . . . My family now . . ."

"And what of children?" Sebastian asked softly. "I expect you'll want a brood."

Joel felt himself frown as he shook his head. "Sometimes *Gott* does not give us what we want."

"Nor should He." Sebastian smiled.

"Why do you say that?"

"Because what we want is not always best for us."

*That's easy for you to say . . . You haven't seen your wife scream, your children buried . . .*

"But you have."

It was a statement, not a question, and Joel had to shake his head to try to figure out if he'd spoken aloud. "What? Did I—I mean—I think I'm overtired. I'll say *gut nacht* now." Joel wanted to run from the barn, from the strange man whom he'd hired without even giving it a second thought. *The man could be evil, or—*

"No." Sebastian laughed ruefully. "Though evil and good are sometimes mistaken for each other."

Joel stared at him in the light of the single kerosene lamp.

168

"You see, Joel, you have been given a great gift."

"I don't know what you're talking about," Joel snapped, suddenly angry without knowing why. "I don't want any gift—any second sight. I've got enough trouble dealing with what I see in the moment." Joel wanted to scream at the *nacht* sky, or call out in fury to *Gott*. He looked at Sebastian, who seemed to be waiting, silently, steadily.

"The gift can be refined, used as a blessing," the *Englischer* said.

Joel pushed past him out of the pen. "I'm tired, Sebastian, and I expect you are too. Get some sleep." He shivered as he left the barn and made for the warmth of the *haus*, unsure whether he had dreamed the last ten minutes or not.

The following morning, Martha let Joel sleep late, wishing there was something more that she might do to help him. But she kept meals hot and ready, cared for the family's needs, and snatched an hour to clean each day as well.

She was dusting the rather large bookshelf in the living area when there was a knock at the door. Puddles raced to get there before her as she hurried lest the visitor awaken Joel. To her surprise, a sturdy-looking teenage Amish girl stood on the porch.

"Frau Umble, your husband hired me to help

you a bit around the *haus* each day. I'm Milly Stolfus."

Martha stood in indecision, considering the girl. While she was grateful to Joel for somehow finding the time to hire help, Martha worried that he felt she couldn't manage the housekeeping on her own. Then she sighed and widened the door. *I might as well be thankful . . .*

Milly came in carrying a wooden bucket filled with cleaning supplies, and Martha gestured to the bookcase. "I was dusting there, if you'd like to continue. And please, Milly, call me Martha."

Milly nodded and went straightaway to the books. Martha pottered about for a few minutes, wanting to make sure that the girl would do all right.

"*Ach*, Martha—what a wealth of books you have." The girl slid one volume from the shelf with visible care. "*Moby Dick*? I love this one— don't you?"

Martha swallowed and stared at the eager young face. "I—I don't . . ." She was saved from a response by Joel's whistling as he entered the room.

He came forward and kissed Martha's cheek, then put a hand on Milly's shoulder. "*Moby Dick*, hmm? I've always thought that 'Call me Ishmael' has got to be one of the best opening lines ever . . ." His deep-throated laughter joined with

Milly's as she agreed and Martha looked on, feeling stupid. And left out.

It wasn't that she hadn't wanted to learn to read and cipher and write her name, but helping around the *haus* and caring for her family had kept her from school. Now she was reminded once again that Joel Umble was far superior to her in learning, and even in thinking. She wondered sadly if it had been truly wise to marry such a man . . .

Another knock on the door broke into her thoughts, and she hurried to open it. May Miller, the healer, stood there with a stack of books in her arms, and Martha had to suppress the sudden urge to scream in frustration.

"Hello, May . . . what have you got there?" Joel moved past Martha to take some of the books from his friend.

May cleared her throat. "I thought, now that you're married, we can stop our poetry reading together."

Joel waved away her words. "*Ach* . . . of course not. In fact, I think it would be *wunderbarr* if Martha joins us." Joel looked to his *frau*, expecting to see a smile in agreement, but instead, he was met by a fierce frown on Martha's lovely mouth.

"Excuse me . . ." Martha murmured. "But I—I have things to do."

Joel watched in confusion as she stalked from the room, and he looked back at May.

"Well, Joel Umble, clearly you messed things up *gut* this time . . ."

He waved May in to make conversation with Milly and went in search of Martha.

He found her standing in their bedroom, looking out of the window. "Martha? Is everything all right?"

"*Jah*," she said softly, turning to him. "What could be wrong?"

He eased the door closed behind him and turned her words over in his mind, trying to pick through her mixed tone. "I have a feeling that means you're really riled up about something."

"Perhaps you do not know me well, Joel Umble . . . Or I you . . ."

He took a few steps toward her, and she visibly tensed. Then he went to the top drawer of the oak dresser near the window. He pulled out a white envelope and handed it to her. "This may be a *gut* time for you to read this . . . It's not great . . . I think I wrote it at four o'clock one morning in the barn, but I hope you'll like it anyway."

He stopped himself from embracing her and slowly made his way back across the room and out the door.

Martha was caught. She held the white envelope between her thumb and forefinger as if it might burn her skin, then finally brought herself to open it. She stared with numb concentration down at the jumble of letters and felt tears fill her eyes. *How can I tell him I cannot read? Surely he will think less of me, realize I am not a proper match for him . . .*

Puddles ran into the room, startling her, and Joel's *mamm* soon followed. Martha hastily wiped at her cheeks and folded the letter, trying to stuff it into her apron pocket.

"What are you hiding there?" Sarah asked.

"*Ach*, it's nothing."

"Looks like a letter," her mother-in-law pointed out, drawing close to Martha. "What does it say?"

Martha wanted to hide, but her kind heart would not let her brush aside this little woman who seemed so anxious and worried about so many things and who had also given Joel life. Martha pulled the letter from her apron and handed it to Sarah. "I don't know what it says. I can't read."

To Martha's surprise, Sarah simply shrugged, then scanned the contents of the letter. "It's a poem for you . . . But if you cannot read, then I will teach you."

Martha stared at the other woman, amazed that such a blessing could *kumme* from admitting the truth about her inabilities. "Joel doesn't know about my lack of reading."

"And why should he?" Sarah gave an unladylike snort. "I can teach you the way I taught both my *sohns*, long before they went to school . . . *Ach*, I do miss Judah, yet I haven't felt like going to the bishop's . . ." Sarah's mood shifted abruptly, and Martha put a strong, young arm around her.

"I'm so very sorry. Perhaps—maybe I can help you, too, Sarah. I know you worry—maybe I can take some of that worry from you by talking whenever you like."

"Perhaps . . . but please, call me Mamm . . ."

# Chapter Twenty-One

Martha was hand-washing clothes with the wringer washer outside on a crisp, sunny day. She didn't care if the clothes stiffened from cold on the lines. She simply rejoiced in keeping things clean and the pleasure of working outside.

She was humming to herself when she happened to look up and see May Miller approaching. Once again, May carried an armful of books, and Martha wished she could simply ignore her. But May stopped next to the washer with a smile on her tanned face.

"Martha—these are the rest of Joel's books. I thought I'd return them."

*Well, they aren't much good to me,* Martha thought, *at least not yet.* "I'll see that he gets them." She took the heavy books and would have turned away from May had the other woman not called her softly.

"Martha?"

"*Jah*?"

"You don't like me much, do you?" May asked with a faint smile.

Martha shifted the weight of the books to her hip and weighed the advantages and hurt feelings that might come if she told the truth. Finally she

175

shrugged. "I don't know you well enough to like or not like you."

"But you think I've got fish hooks into your husband, right? You feel that because we used to read together that maybe there were other things we did together, hmmm?"

"Well," Martha said flatly. "Yes."

May sighed. "I was married once—to a man who was a monster—but I escaped and made a new life on Ice Mountain. I do not want any romantic entanglements with anyone. Now, is Joel Umble fine to look at in face and form? Of course. But I would not take your husband or anyone else's. I want to focus on my work as a healer."

Martha recognized the sincerity in May's words and felt herself begin to relax. "Um . . . would you . . . do you want to come in for some tea?"

"Some other day, perhaps—and I'd like it very much, Martha, if you'd find your way to my cabin if you'd ever like to talk."

Martha laughed. "Without Joel?"

"Without Joel!"


Later that day, Joel came in from the sheepfold to find Martha scrubbing the kitchen floor while Milly Loftus did the dishes. He pulled Martha to her feet and bade Milly to see to the needs of the family for an hour.

"We're going to Sol Kauffman's store," he announced, steering Martha out the back door.

"*Ach*, but Joel, I don't have a proper dress—it's patched, and I look—"

"Beautiful," he whispered against the soft skin of her cheek. "And I've tended enough ewes this year to last a lifetime. Now it's time I see that my wife is dressed with care and also has whatever her heart may desire."

"I have everything I desire," she mumbled.

Joel smiled. "Me too, but I do think that a few yards of fabric won't hurt you any."

He led her through the wooded paths that went to Sol's store. He put an arm around her slender waist as they mounted the five stone steps and entered the store with a cheerful accompaniment of the bells that rang whenever the door moved.

Joel could tell when she straightened her spine that some of the people who looked down on Martha and the Yoders were inside the store. He knew his young wife had more soul beauty than any woman present. And present were the Raber sisters. Joel kept his arm around Martha as Ruby flounced toward him.

"Joel Umble, what are these rumors the grapevine tells?" She pointedly ignored Martha, and Joel smiled widely.

"I believe you know my wife, Martha. Martha, you recall Ruby Raber?"

Martha nodded politely while Ruby was forced to reluctantly nod at the newest member of the Umble family.

"You'll have to excuse us, Ruby. We've got a bunch of shopping to do." And, indeed, Sol Kauffman called out Joel's name and motioned Martha and him to the back counter of the store.

"Joel, bring your bride! Let me give a gift to you both." Sol set a huge circular object on the wooden counter. "See? Just right, I say."

"*Ach,*" Martha exclaimed before Joel could even reply. "A wheel of smoked cheese! *Wunderbarr!*"

"*Jah.*" Sol extended a hamlike hand to Martha. "*Schmart* woman you are, Martha Umble, to know that smoked cheese is a wonderful thing!"

Joel smiled at the gift, but then his eyes strayed to the dry goods section of the store.

Sol's *dochder*, Lucy, was a big, comfortable-looking girl who smiled on them with visible excitement. She was waiting with her shears on the other side of the wooden counter, which was notched to indicate yardage, and leaned across to whisper conspiratorially. "Heard about the marriage. Congratulations."

Martha nodded, her throat feeling dry. She knew what it was to come in to Sol's store with less than five cents, and the prospect of shopping for dress material left her feeling nervous. But Joel was smiling, clearly happy that she might

178

have some new things. She decided to be brave for his sake.

It had been a long while since she had purchased anything like the makings for a new dress, but she had a keen eye for color and was an excellent seamstress, thanks to her *grossmuder*'s teaching. So she directed Lucy cautiously to pull down a bolt of forest green, as well as one of a rich burgundy color.

"These are pretty, Joel," she murmured softly.

He smiled down at her. "Indeed they are, but please, sweetheart, choose many more."

"He's right, Martha Umble," Lucy said as she came around the counter to briefly measure Martha's waist. "Better to have an extra dress or two, because likely the pair of you will be asked all around the mountain to celebrate your marriage."

Martha nodded and noticed Joel staring up at the rainbow of colors. "Was there something you liked?" she asked hesitantly.

His teeth flashed white for a second, and he bent close to her ear. "*Jah*, the wedding blue, Martha. Why should you not have the dress of a bride when that's what you are in truth?"

"*Ach* . . . if you'd like." She chose a light blue and then folded her hands and stepped back from the counter as Lucy applied her shears with a ready expertise.

Martha watched in fascination as each piece

of fabric was wrapped carefully in brown paper and tied with string, but she was appalled at the cost when they stood once again at the counter by Sol's cash drawer. She tugged on Joel's sleeve as he paid, and he looked at her with a raised eyebrow.

"Joel, *sei se gut*, this is all wonderful, but isn't it—well, a bit costly?"

He hugged her close and kissed her temple. "You are worth costly things, Martha, and besides, remember, I know you didn't marry me for my money."

She swatted him lightly on the arm for his joking, then simply rejoiced in the feel of his strength around her. Little did she know, but their casual and tender way with each other assured many more than the jealous Ruby Raber that theirs was a love match and meant to last.

As was common on Ice Mountain in the spring, a sudden thunderstorm brewed up and caught them with their packages on the way back. They had to run the last few yards, getting wet and breathless together.

They blew in through the back door, laughing, while Milly Loftus looked on with a faintly indulgent air. Joel took the brown paper–wrapped packages from Martha and kissed her quickly on the lips. He noticed her blush and appreciated the rosy hue, thinking that he'd also enjoy seeing such a flush over the expanse of her throat and breasts.

But he drew himself up sharply and left the kitchen, whistling in cheerful tones.

Martha sent Milly to fold the wash, which the girl had managed to get in before the storm, and set about making some sandwiches for her family and Sarah. She hummed softly to herself as she worked, praising *Gott* for the amount of food available. She listened to the rolling thunder and crashes of lightning with pleasure, always having enjoyed hearing a storm.

When she heard a knock at the back door, she turned from the table. She wondered who might be out in such weather and quickly moved to raise the latch to give the person shelter. But Judah loomed up before her, tall and menacing, his eerie face and dull eyes illuminated by the violent flashes of lightning. She opened her mouth to scream and he moved fast and clamped a cruel hand across her lips. Martha struggled furiously, knowing Joel was somewhere in the *haus*. But Judah's strength was far greater than her own, and he pulled her outside into the storm and flung her down on the muddy ground. She blinked in the heavy rain and tried to rise, but Judah fell full length upon her and clamped his mouth to hers, nearly suffocating her, and effectively silencing her scream . . .

• • •

Joel came back into the kitchen and stared, perplexed, at the screen door standing wide open. He walked out onto the porch and scanned the ground before his eyes landed on a blue-and-white bundle against the rain-pelted earth.

"Martha!" He ran to her and fell on his knees beside her. "Martha, are you hurt? Can you hear me?"

He scooped her up and carried her inside to the living area and laid her gently on the soft couch, heedless of the water and mud that covered her. She opened her eyes slowly as he spoke to her and wiped her face with the end of his shirt. Her mouth was bleeding, and a heavy bruise was beginning to swell her right eye.

"Martha?" He didn't want to upset her, but he had to know what had happened. "Who did this to you?"

"Judah," she whispered softly, then reached her arms to hug her body protectively.

"Did he—"

She shook her head weakly. "He . . . hit me. Then suddenly ran off."

Joel's mouth tightened. He gestured for Milly Loftus, who had hurried to get a small basin and cloth, to come closer. "Stay with her, Milly, please, and don't alarm the rest of the family, *sei se gut*. I must *geh* and find my *bruder*."

Martha caught his arm with dirty, slender fingers. "Please, Joel. Don't *geh* . . ."

He gently loosened her grasp and bent to kiss her forehead. "I must, Martha. I will *kumme* back."

He recognized the acceptance in her eyes and quickly set out on foot to hunt for Judah. His first impulse was to go to the bishop's *haus*, but something in him said that Judah wouldn't be there. Instead, he followed his brother's tracks away from the place where Martha had lain, winding deeper and deeper, up and into the forest.

Joel's breathing grew harsh as he ran in the pounding rain. The roar of the thunder rivaled the noise of his heart pounding, but he kept on, determined to finally have things out with Judah.

He'd reached the high timber and was tracking mostly on instinct, because the rain had pounded away any footprints. He rounded a wide-girthed maple and nearly ran full tilt into his *bruder* as he knelt on the ground with his head bent upward as if in appeal to the heavens.

Without preamble, Joel tackled Judah, feeling a satisfying grunt of pain come from his older brother. It didn't matter at that moment that an Amish man was not supposed to engage in violence toward another—let alone his brother. Joel was past caring. He landed another blow on Judah's face.

"As if I'd let you strike my wife!" Joel roared over the rain, getting to his feet.

Judah laughed, and something cold grew in Joel's heart, fast sprouting to maturity.

"You're a fool, little *bruder*!" Judah taunted, despite the punching he was taking.

"And you, Judah, are evil . . . but why? Why?" Joel stopped and staggered backward, trying to catch his breath. The rain slowed, but the thunder and lightning continued, adding a sinister fogginess to the scene.

Blood and rain ran down Judah's face, and Joel looked away for a second, only to turn back in time to see Judah rear upward over him with the glint of a large hunting knife in his hand. Joel had braced for the blow when lightning struck the knife and then Judah, running to ground in the small puddle of water he stood in. Judah gave an agonized cry, then fell down upon the wet earth, his hand still clutching the knife.

Joel lost all his anger at the thought of Judah being badly hurt or worse . . . He waited until he judged it to be safe to get close to his brother, then looked into Judah's eyes. Somehow, the brown depths had lost their coldness, their deathlike focus, and Joel could only wonder at the change he saw. Judah slowly dropped the knife and, with his other hand, reached out to Joel.

Joel took Judah's hand and started to speak softly as the thunder finally rolled away. "I'll get you home, Judah."

"Na—na—no, just listen ta me."

"I'm listening." Joel bent near.

"I—thought—ta save—Martha. Wr—wrong."

Joel nodded, struggling to understand his brother's nerve-damaged speech.

"Ya—you think to safe—save her too." Judah smiled gently. "You wrong too."

Joel shook his head in mute denial, thinking about the vision of the tombstones.

"Cannot change—future—Jo-Joel. Not yours ta—change."

"Okay—okay, Judah. Save your strength. I'll carry you home."

"Will—di—die here. Read—jour-journal and beware of—bish—bishop . . ." Judah's head tilted to one side, and Joel watched the life seep out of his brother's eyes as if it were draining into the ground. Joel bowed his head and prayed.

# Chapter Twenty-Two

That *nacht*, Martha sat up in bed, waiting to turn down the lantern, until Joel came to bed. She tried to shut her ears to the sobbing she could hear—Sarah Umble crying for her eldest *sohn*. Martha felt tears tremble on her own lashes. She knew that the time appointed for Judah to die had *kumme* from *Gott*, but she couldn't help but feel that she held some guilt in the whole thing. She tried to pray and was glad when Joel finally came to *geh* to sleep.

"Still up?" he asked softly, coming to sit on the edge of the bed beside her. "Did the ice help your eye any?"

Martha shrugged, then impulsively caught his hand in hers. "Joel—I'm sorry."

"You're sorry? Whatever for?" He leaned close to gather her in his arms with great tenderness. "You were victimized by Judah—hurt by him over and over—but you did nothing to cause that."

She nodded in agreement, though she felt like it was to soothe Joel more than herself. Then she looked into his dark blue eyes and saw the great burden of pain he carried.

"*Ach*, Joel—you did nothing either."

"I want to believe that as truth." He leaned

forward and kissed her cheek with slow warmth. "I'm tired, sweetheart. Do you mind if we turn down the lamp?"

He rose from the bed, and she had a brief image of him lowering his suspenders before the room was engulfed in darkness.

Judah's death garnered much sympathy from the community, as any death would. As he prepared for the funeral, Joel found himself missing his shunned best friend, Stephen. Joel decided that he'd make a trip up to Stephen's cabin as soon as he was able.

Joel had told Martha that she needed to stay home from the funeral and rest. He wasn't sure what Bishop Loftus might say at the graveside, and he didn't want to expose Martha to any further pain.

The graveside ceremony would be a traditional Amish funeral. The body had been dressed and prepared by friends of the family, and Joel led the men bearing the wooden coffin on their shoulders. It struck his spirit hard that he bore his *bruder*'s corpse on his back. The finality of Judah's death seemed to bear down upon him. He'd never truly understood why there was such discord between them during life, and now there would be no opportunity to mend it.

They soon arrived at the cemetery, and Joel

looked away for a moment from the even rows of tombstones—they reminded him too much of his vision. And then his thoughts nettled him— *What had Judah said? That I can't save Martha either . . .*

He helped lower the casket to the portable stand that had been erected beside the open grave. Then the top half of the coffin was opened on hinges so that those who wished might file past and see Judah's face one last time.

Joel offered his *mamm* his arm, meaning to give her something to lean on as she walked, but she stiffened and refused, walking instead alone and on shaky feet.

When the last of the community had looked upon Judah, the casket was closed and Bishop Loftus began to speak.

"It is not often that I have had to bury so young a man, so gentle in spirit, so full of *Gott*'s possibilities . . ."

Joel struggled to control a sudden cough. *In what way had Judah been full of* Gott? Joel's anger simmered at the back of his mind. He realized that he'd been enraged with his *bruder* for years because of Judah's cruelty and carelessness. And the very one Joel had wanted to protect—Martha—had suffered the most because of Judah. *I am not sorry he's dead . . . He can do no more harm to Martha . . .*

The bishop's words suddenly broke into his

thoughts, and Joel listened in growing disbelief and fury.

"No doubt many of you gathered here understand that those who've been impoverished by *Derr Herr* for their sins cannot truly hope to improve their circumstance on the back of an upright man. This is only a temporary haven that soon will be destroyed by *Gott*'s Own Hand. And we should not be deceived by pretty words and looks! *Nee* . . . because the Bible speaks to the fact that even Satan can still appear as an Angel of Light. So be on guard, my friends, that you do not meet the same end as dear Judah, who only sought to banish what was impure from among us."

Joel lifted his gaze to meet the bishop's shark eyes squarely. He nodded slowly at the older man in open challenge, knowing that such lies could not *geh* on unchecked . . .

Martha was surprised to discover Sarah Umble sitting with her parents one morning when she went to give them breakfast. Up until now, she'd thought that her mother-in-law would rather prefer to be alone.

"Martha." Her *mamm*'s soft voice broke into her thoughts, and she smiled readily.

"*Jah*, Mamm and Daed. And my new—*mamm*." She put down the loaded tray on a round table that was near the window in the large, pleasant room. "Is anyone hungry?"

"Always, Dochder," Chet Yoder said in a cheery tone, and Martha's smile widened.

It was rare to find her *fater* in such *gut* humor, but then, she had not spent that much time with him lately beyond seeing to his care.

"*Jah*, yer *mamm* and I are enjoyin' the company of this fine lady. She's got a ready sense of humor that does a body *gut*."

Martha gazed with wonder for a brief second at Sarah Umble. *A ready sense of humor? I must spend more time with her . . . I guess I've been hiding from her in a way, since Judah . . .*

Martha set up trays and plates and adjusted pillows to maximum comfort. She was about to ask Sarah if she might bring her something, when that woman chirped up.

"Sit down, girl. You're making my nerves ache with all of your moving about. Hand me a piece of bacon and tell your parents a *gut* joke."

Martha dropped obediently into a chair, passed the plate of bacon to her mother-in-law and wracked her brains for some kind of joke. "Well," she said finally. "I can tell you a tale of a pig named Phillipe . . ."

For days, Bishop Loftus's words gnawed at Joel. He went through the motions of daily living, but knew himself to be distant and removed, and that was the last thing he wanted to be with Martha.

The spring chores about the farm kept him

occupied, and he found that Martha's interest in the kitchen garden was something that gave him moments of joy. He and Sebastian had turned a great deal larger plot of land than had been done in years past. Usually, a sustainable garden meant only plowing the minimum amount of footage for each person in the *haus*, but Martha insisted that the garden should have edible flowers, pumpkins, and herbs, in addition to the regular crops.

"I've never thought about edible flowers," Joel had to confess as he and Martha left the *haus* early one morning to plan the layout of the flower section.

"Perhaps there is much you have not thought of, Joel Umble," Martha said saucily, flashing him a smile that made him feel warm as toast inside.

He caught her close when they were outside. "There are some things that I can recall, now that you mention it." He kissed her gently, with great tenderness, and she responded with an intensity that shook him.

When he finally pulled away, he saw that she was already two steps ahead, her bare toes digging deep in the rich, loosened earth. He had a sudden image of what a daughter of Martha's would be like—all brown braids and bare feet, running wild on the mountain.

He had to shake himself from his imagining as the vision of the tombstones reared up ir his mind, and he told himself fiercely to stop daydreaming.

He followed Martha more soberly now, but her enthusiasm was hard to resist.

"*Ach*, Joel, Grossmuder has some heirloom seeds that she's kept from last year in her button box. I hope that we will have *gut* crops of sweet cicely, thyme, lemon mint, and borage."

"All right. I don't know half of what you've just said, but it sounds *gut*."

She spread her arms wide and made small motions with her hands like a master conductor warming up an orchestra. He began to see her vision for the simple earth that lay before them.

"We need fennel, nasturtium, pineapple sage, and roses—lots of roses!"

He caught her close once more, staring down into her bright face. "*Ach*, Martha, you do a heart *gut*."

"Do I, Joel?"

Her lashes lowered and he saw a hectic flush of color come into her cheeks. The urge to kiss her was strong, but he turned from her instead, muttering about nonexistent chores that had to be done with the sheep.

# Chapter Twenty-Three

Martha sighed to herself and tried for the third time to focus on Sarah Umble's teaching of the letters in the simple child's primer. It was bright and sunny out and Martha would have rather been in the garden planting her seeds. Though when she'd been outside with Joel that morning, he'd seemed to be all too willing to escape her nearness. Indeed, since Judah's death, Joel had been distant, when he wasn't kissing her, and she found his behavior to be perplexing.

"The letters on the page, girl," Sarah snapped. "Not what's out the window!"

Martha jumped and refocused her attention. She and Sarah only had time to study here and there, and Martha despaired of ever gaining enough skill to read Joel's letter. Still, she was a diligent student most of the time and had made progress.

Now she glanced over the page to discreetly study Sarah, who seemed to spend more and more time with either Martha's *grossmuder* or her parents lately. Joel's *mamm* had even ceased much of her anxious behavior in the past days, and Martha wondered if the uniting of the two families of older folks might not be a benefit all of them.

"The page, girl!"

Martha giggled and began to sound out the letters she knew.

"Now, what is it you're wanting to order, Joel Umble?" Sol Kauffman stood with pen poised over an order form while Joel whispered once more what he wanted to have sent up the mountain.

"Three wheelchairs . . . for Martha's family. I want them to be as padded and comfortable as possible. I think if they can easily go outside, the fresh air will do her family a world of *gut*."

Sol grunted as he scribbled, then looked up with a sudden gleam in his eyes. "*Kumme* with me, *buwe*. Lucy! Mind the store. I'm going out to the back barn for a minute."

Joel followed the tall man out through the back of the store, which was attached to the family's living area. They walked to one of the larger barns on the property, and Sol lit a lantern to illuminate the dim interior.

Pigeons had roosted here and there and the cow stalls were empty and abandoned, proof of a different time, when the store had not been the family's business.

"Now . . ." Sol led the way up to the haymows nd then poked about in a dark corner. He lifted tarp from something, then smiled heartily. ere!"

Joel peered into the gloom and was amazed at what he saw.

"Why is it here?"

"Polio," Sol said with a sudden dark look. "Me own *grossmuder* was bound to the thing, but I wager we can fix it up to give Martha's family some freedom right away. And I'll order you two more of the new-fangled ones to be brought up the mountain."

Joel clapped the older man on the shoulder. "*Danki*, Sol. *Danki* . . ."

Martha watched in fascination as Joel and Sebastian fitted wood planks together after having removed one set of the front steps from the *haus*. She paused with a packet of seeds in her hand and couldn't resist watching the play of muscle and sinew across Joel's back. He was as beautiful as any wild thing, and she longed for their so-called courtship to be at end so that she could claim him as the lover of her heart.

She sat down idly on the edge of the porch, and Sebastian suggested that he *geh* and get some more wood, leaving Martha alone with her husband.

Joel glanced up at her, and she saw the blaze of his eyes as they trailed down the considerable length of bare leg she displayed as she sat.

"It grows warmer each day," she commented.

"*Jah* . . ." he replied absently, still much involved with studying her.

She gave a delicate stretch, knowing his eyes followed the press of her breasts against the apron of her dress. "I think, Joel Umble, that I will forgo the bathtub tonight and bathe in the creek. Would you care to join me?"

She saw the rigid set of his shoulders and knew what he would say before he spoke. She bounced to her feet and didn't wait to hear him but rather headed for the kitchen garden.

She knelt and began to sow some ghost tomatoes, telling herself that she was comfortable in the garden and that it didn't matter if Joel didn't want to lie with her. She glanced up suddenly as a shadow fell over her and she saw Joel standing near the row she was working on. "What is it?" she asked, using her hand to shield her eyes from the sun.

He knelt in the dirt next to her, and she caught the rich manly scent of him, part pine soap and part sunshine.

"It seems I've given you the idea that I don't desire you, Martha Umble."

"Well . . ." She gulped back a sob. "Maybe you don't."

She felt him cup gentle hands about her face, and then he was kissing her in long, sultry pulls. He used his tongue and gentle nips of his teeth until she forgot her tears and was kissing him back with ardor, willing to have him make love to her right in the middle of the fresh field.

"I will see you for your bath tonight, sweetheart," he whispered against her throat.

She smiled against his lips and knew a moment of true joy.

Joel avoided Sebastian's thoughtful gaze for the rest of the afternoon. But finally, before supper, he grew exasperated and turned from his ramp building to face the *Englischer*.

"All right, Sebastian . . . out with it, if you please."

"I'm just thinking, that's all," the other man replied with his slow smile.

"About what?" Joel snapped, feeling petty but seeing no help for it.

"This working on an Amish farm has me thinking that I'd like to start and keep a journal—about our day-to-day experiences, how the sheep fare, what it's like to watch a garden grow—"

"Wait." Joel stopped him with a raised hand, tilting his head to one side as if listening to something far away. "What did you say?"

"A journal—like you write in . . ."

"I know. I know." Joel slowly lowered the hammer he was using. "Judah said something about a journal. I'd forgotten it until now. He said something about . . . rcading a journal . . . telling me to do it and to beware the bishop all in one breath."

"Well, maybe Judah kept a journal," Sebastian suggested.

"I've never looked at Judah's things. The bishop just returned a chest of them, and I carted it off to the attic. So it wouldn't upset Mamm lying around."

Sebastian shrugged. "Maybe it would be worth taking a look."

Joel got to his feet, feeling compelled. "I think I will, Sebastian. Thanks."

Martha sat back on her knees, sorting seeds on the floor in her *grossmuder*'s bright room. The *auld* lady had asked if a flower garden might not be planted directly outside her window, and Martha had loved the idea.

"How about yellow lady's slipper?"

"*Jah.*" Her *grossmuder* smiled. "They do indeed look beautiful, and are as delicate as the dancing shoe of any fine lady."

Martha nodded. "And some Carolina lupine and merrybells . . . *Ach*, and what about some maidenhair ferns and the woodland iris?"

"You're spoiling me, girlie," Esther Yoder quipped.

Martha moved to sit in the rocking chair near the *auld* lady's bed. She put out a strong, young hand to cover the aged, blue-veined hands of her *grossmuder*. "Tell me a story," Martha suggested cheerfully.

Her *grossmuder* smiled. "Now, you haven't asked for that since you were a wee one. Why do you ask today?"

Martha smiled readily and answered with truth. "*Ach*, because I love your stories, and perhaps because I want the day to pass more quickly . . ."

"So you can spend some time alone with Joel Umble?"

Martha blushed faintly. "*Jah*."

Esther Yoder smiled and leaned back against the comfortable mound of white pillows behind her. "Well, for your truthfulness, I'll give you a story. An *auld* tale, but entertaining nonetheless . . . Let's see, girlie. My husband, your *grossdaddi*, died a long while ago, though I miss him still. But he and I got to be friends with an *Englisch* couple named Dutch and Hazel Wolfe. Dutch would *geh* hunting with your grand*fater* and Hazel would teach me fancy work called crocheting. Anyway, girlie, there was something folks said was odd about Dutch. He was *auld* even when we knew him and wore this jaunty hat on his bald head. His face looked like a raisin, it was so wrinkled . . . But Dutch had this Bible, and he'd bid you to try and open it, and you would try and try and it was as if the pages were glued tight. But you'd hand it back to Dutch, and he'd open it just fine."

"A trick?" Martha asked.

"*Nee*. Because when *auld* Dutch read the Good Book, the pages moved just fine. Some called Dutch a hex, yet he showed nothing but kindness to us. I remember once, when your *daed* was small and having *nacht*mares about something or another, that Dutch came into the *haus* and took a broom he had and went along and swept the ceiling of the room. He swept it clean like it was a kitchen floor. Then he told your *fater* that he would have no more bad dreams, that he'd swept them all away. And . . . your *fater* never did again."

Martha was enchanted. "What else did Dutch do?"

"Well, it was said that Dutch knew a verse in Leviticus in the Bible that could stop a man from bleeding. Sure enough, your grandfather invited Dutch and some other men to *geh* in a hunting party for grouse. Well, one man got loose with the trigger and shot another fella right in the chest. Your *grossdaddi* said that it was bad and that the man was sure to bleed to death before they could get him to a doctor, but then Dutch knelt down beside him and said the verse from the Bible, and the bleeding stopped. It stopped long enough for the men to get him a doctor, and he eventually recovered—thanks to *Derr Herr* and Dutch."

Her grandmother's voice died off softly.

"What happened to Dutch?"

"*Ach*, girlie, he died, same as everybody else

is bound to do, and he asked that his Bible be buried with him and it was. Yep, that was the last of Dutch in this world."

There was a certain sadness that hung in the room, and Martha sought to banish it by going back to the seeds, but not before she'd kissed her *grossmuder*'s cheek with tenderness and thanked her for the story.

Joel eased open his *bruder*'s trunk as he knelt in the attic of the *haus*. He felt odd, touching Judah's things, almost as if Judah himself stood nearby. Then Joel shrugged off the melancholy feeling and carefully laid each item on the floor beside him. There were clothes and shoes and knives—Judah's hunting guns were downstairs in a glass-fronted cabinet. There was a metal deer drag, his pocket watch, and a few bits of coin. *That's all . . . all that a man's life comes down to, and none of it he could take in his coffin with him . . . But what's missing?*

"What is missing?" Joel said aloud. Then he realized that not only was there no sign of a journal but that Judah's Bible was also absent. It was odd, because Judah usually carried the dark-covered Bible with him . . . He put all of the things back and decided that perhaps Judah had been delirious with pain when he'd mentioned a journal—but Joel would certainly heed his warning to beware of Bishop Loftus.

201

# Chapter Twenty-Four

Martha shivered a bit, but not with the cold. She was nervous lest Joel forget to come. Or perhaps he had simply changed his mind about joining her for a bath in the creek. She'd brought fluffy white towels from the *haus* and had followed the water back to the woods and the secret pool where she and Joel had met that moonlit *nacht*.

After a few discouraging minutes, Martha decided that she might as well take advantage of the chill water and started to unbind her hair. But then she turned suddenly, having the oddest feeling that she was being watched.

"Joel?"

Only the light wind answered her, and she decided to shrug off her imaginings. Quickly, she stripped down and made the first bone-chilling plunge into the creek hole. She came up gasping, only to see Joel standing on the creek bank before her.

"Joel Umble! You scared me half to death . . . Were you watching me earlier?"

"*Nee.*" He knelt down on the bank. "I just got here. I'm watching you now, though."

Her lips curled in a soft smile. "So you are. Do you need help getting undressed?"

He shook his head and got back to his feet. His

hat and coat were off quickly but then he took his time lowering his suspenders and unpinning his burgundy shirt.

Even in the filtered light of the moon, she thought his chest looked beautiful—supple skin, well defined, with an arrow of dark hair that ran interestingly downward to disappear beneath the waistband of his wool pants.

Martha was completely charmed at the sight and waited for him to continue . . .

Joel decided he was definitely having fun. It was a joy to have his wife's rapt, wide-eyed attention. But it was even more pleasurable when he eased himself into the icy coldness of the creek and then caught Martha close to him. The multiple sensations of rushing water, swirling stimulation, and the feel of her body clasped to his were exhilarating. He started kissing her, finding the honeyed warmth of her mouth and plunging his tongue inside again and again to duel with her own. She curled clever fingers up to pull the hair at the nape of his neck, and he closed his eyes with pleasure when she slid her hands lower. When he lifted his head to catch his breath, he found her eyes dazed in response to his actions.

"I never knew I could feel like that," she said, and he smiled, preparing to repeat her pleasure.

But the snap of a branch made him turn suddenly, scanning the bank. He enclosed Martha in the fold of his arms, wondering if it might be a stray black bear come out of its den.

"Come on." He started to pull her from the water.

"What is it?"

"Probably nothing, but I'd like you to *geh* back home. I want to have a look around after I dress." She looked as though she might protest, but then she nodded and climbed the bank, wrapping herself in one of the thick towels.

Joel did the same. "*Kumme*, I'll see you to the edge of the woods."

They were silent as they walked, and he kissed her quickly once they'd cleared the tree line, then he watched her run safely to the lamps of the *haus*. Then he turned back to the forest and began to wind his way back to the creek's pool, not sure what he was looking for, but intent just the same.

Joel started when another tall figure suddenly loomed up before him in the half light of the moon.

"Stephen!" he exclaimed, not expecting to see his shunned friend.

"Joel—what are you about in the woods this late?"

"Were you just back by the bathing pool in the creek?"

Stephen's handsome mouth curved in a grin. "Spying on the newly married? *Nee* . . . I was coming back from taking some fish to my *mamm* and *aenti*'s *haus*. Why do you ask?"

Joel shrugged. "I don't know—I just felt— well, never mind. Probably an overactive mind."

"Or an overexcited husband?"

Joel threw an arm about his friend's shoulders. "*Kumme* for a cup of coffee, why don't you? I miss your dry wit!"

But Stephen shook his dark head. "*Nee* . . . I'd better get back to the cabin. But Joel, my *mamm* told me of Judah—I am sorry for your loss."

"*Danki*, friend. He was—a troubled soul. But . . . I'd better head home. I'll *kumme* up to hunt with you soon."

"As long as Loftus is bishop, you'd better not socialize with a shunned man."

Joel laughed wryly. "I'll socialize with whoever I want. *Gut nacht*."

"*Gut nacht* . . . and be careful out here."

Joel watched Stephen walk off, then decided he'd head back home. He had probably heard nothing . . .

Martha slid the blue garter Mrs. Ellis had given her up the length of her leg with trembling fingers. She settled its pretty rosette and lace around her lower thigh, then pulled on the short peach-colored gown that she'd bought at Nancy's Niceties in Coudersport. Thus dressed, or rather undressed, she turned down the lanterns in the master bedroom to give off a warm and soothing light. Then she stood waiting, trying to curb her anxiousness. Perhaps he'd think her too bold or overly wanton, but she wanted an end to Joel's idea of courtship.

She threw her shoulders back and stood tall as the latch rattled on the door. Joel entered with his head down, so he didn't see her at first but then he lifted his gaze, and Martha wet her lips, wondering how he'd respond . . .

Joel stood transfixed, his eyes taking in the loveliness of his wife. She wore a short, transparent gown that was more alluring than bare flesh and a pale blue frilly thing that brought his attention to the suppleness of her long legs.

He shut the door behind him with tingling fingers and took a step toward her, not trusting himself to speak at first.

"My hair is still damp from the creek," she said in normal tones, tossing the mass over her shoulder and back.

He envied her calm; he was shaken to his very core with the measure of her beauty. Her white throat was laid bare, and her round breasts strained at the thin fabric, while her narrow waist and full hips seemed to beckon to him.

"Martha," he said, his voice husky with feeling. "You're so beautiful."

"Please, Joel. Please make love to me."

He nodded despite himself and crossed the floor in two long strides. He slipped one arm around her waist and the other beneath her knees. Then he swung her up eagerly and carried her to the bed.

They tumbled together on the turned-down sheets and Joel ran his hands up and down her lush frame while she eagerly sought the damp edges of his shirt and helped him ease it off. Her kisses caused a fine sheen of perspiration on his body, and he tugged hard at the hook and eye of his black pants, feeling the stitches give way. Then he lay between her thighs and it seemed the most natural thing in the world until his brain kicked in . . . *No child . . . no child . . .* He lifted his hips and moved hard against her belly. Once . . . twice . . . and then he heard his own sobbing release, but he knew that he had left Martha behind in his eagerness.

Martha blinked as she felt a curious wetness between her body and Joel's. He had pulled back and was hastily sliding up his pants and then got up to walk across the room to the bowl and pitcher. She watched him wash unabashedly, knowing that the pleasure she had felt could not soften the meaning of his movements. He wanted no child with her. She didn't know whether to rage or cry. Then her typical common sense took over and she told herself that perhaps he wanted to give them some time alone as a couple . . . She settled on this explanation, though a vague fear still gnawed at her.

Joel came back to bed and gathered her close, and she nestled against his broad shoulder. He didn't speak, and Martha couldn't, either, so she simply listened to the even cadence of his breathing until she fell asleep.

# Chapter Twenty-Five

Joel had grown used to the seemingly boundless energy that Sebastian displayed in his work about the farm, and he had come to rely on the *Englischer* a great deal. Joel was grateful for Sebastian especially when it came time for shearing the sheep. He had been pleasantly surprised to discover that Sebastian was familiar with sheep. The man said he'd sheared many a time.

Shearing was not for amateurs. If a person didn't go about things right, the fleece, that one whole piece of the sheep's coat, could be ruined, and moreover, the sheep would run around looking like it'd had a bad haircut. Joel had even learned over the years that the other sheep would seem to mock a badly shaven sheep by baaing at it or giving it little nips on its blotchy pink skin. So Joel was always careful to keep every sheep looking as uniform to the others as possible.

He and Sebastian set up a table and a small pen and went to the task with handheld sheep shears.

"We might do better with an set of electric shears," Sebastian joked as the day grew hotter and the shearing seemed to drag on.

Joel laughed good-naturedly, then looked up

as Martha came across the field carrying a metal pail. Her green dress was beautiful and her hair properly braided beneath her *kapp*, but Joel could still see her in the peach *nacht*gown and had to shake himself to greet her with a lopsided smile.

"I made some lemonade," she called and both men stopped what they were doing for a taste of the lemony goodness with its hint of sugar.

Joel bent to kiss her to convey his thanks, and she smiled and nodded before walking away. Joel watched her for a long moment, then turned back to find Sebastian with a faint smile on his face.

"What?" Joel asked.

"Young love," Sebastian returned.

They both laughed, but Joel felt something deep within his spirit. *Young love . . . Do I love Martha? Of course . . .* But the thought stuck with him that he'd rarely if ever told her that he loved her . . . Suddenly the sheep-shearing seemed to fly by as he noticed that his heart felt full and the colors of the earth seemed brighter. And he knew that he'd write Martha another letter as soon as he could.

Martha knelt on the expanse of hardwood floor in her parents' bedroom. She'd just *kumme* in from taking Joel some lemonade and had decided to use the rest of the afternoon until supper in sewing a new dress. Sarah Umble was there to help, too, and the time seemed jolly as they worked together. Even her *fater* helped by dutifully holding out the pincushion.

The new dress was to be burgundy—a color that Joel seemed to favor himself.

"*Ach*, but it's nice to have something to sew on again," Elise Yoder said, her still pretty face wreathed in smiles. Martha returned her *mamm*'s gentle look, glad that here, too, was a blessing from marrying Joel. Her mother seemed more relaxed in the warm, new *haus* and less prone to her asthma attacks.

Martha pinned and sewed the dress bodice front to its matching back piece at the shoulders. Then she obediently stood on a small wooden stool while Sarah measured and pinned the sleeves. Elise quickly hemmed the two lengths to the proper measurement, and Martha went on to pin and sew pleats into the skirt front and back pieces and into the apron. She knew at this point that some Amish from off the mountain would also sew a cape to the shoulders, but Ice Mountain Amish were not so fancy. Next came the apron, and the stiffening needed to be sewn into the belt—this was a tricky piece of work that Martha managed quickly and neatly.

As she worked, she thought of Joel and their lovemaking the *nacht* before. It was therefore a surprise when she came back to the moment to hear her *mamm*'s gentle voice.

"Perhaps one day soon, we will be sewing for a baby."

Martha bit her lip, not wanting to give her mother the wrong idea, but she couldn't help the words that tumbled out. "But, Mamm, we've only been married a short time."

"Plenty of time to make a baby," Sarah remarked, causing Martha to blush.

"I'm nearly finished here. What's something special that I can make for Joel's dinner, since he's been working so hard?" She was relieved that she was able to come up with a thought to change the course of the conversation.

"Stuffed meat loaf," her *fater* said promptly, waving the pincushion for emphasis.

"Mashed potatoes, gravy, corn, and something for dessert," Sarah chimed in.

"Mayonnaise cake?" her *mamm* offered and Martha nodded.

"All right," Martha smiled. "I'll clean up here and then get to work!"

Joel sat in the sunshine on an *auld* picnic bench. The shearing had been accomplished, and he had a few minutes to jot down some thoughts for Martha. It was easier for him somehow to write what he was feeling than speak directly to her. He supposed that it had always been that way, when his gifts to his *mamm* on various occasions had been handwritten cards and the like. But

212

he struggled now, unsure of how to explain to Martha how much she meant to him.

A persistent whine broke into his thoughts, and he looked up to see an unfamiliar little dog, its white fur splotched by mud and its plumy tail wagging in faint hopefulness.

Joel patted his leg and tried an experimental call to the animal. The little dog bounded to him and promptly jumped into Joel's lap.

"Why, hello . . . Hello there, little friend. Let's see if you have a collar under that mud . . . Nope. Well, you're welcome here."

The dog seemed to sense its change of circumstances and licked Joel's cheek appreciatively. Joel smiled, hoping Martha liked animals. He'd always wanted a dog to help him herd sheep, but Judah had presented an obstacle. His brother had had no softness for animals.

"Let's get you cleaned up and we'll *geh* and see the lady of the *haus*."

The little dog happily accompanied him to the creek and, once bathed, turned out to be pure white with a nice pink belly. Joel scooped her up into his arms once more. "All right, little one, let's *geh* home."

Martha was making stuffing. It was rather tedious an affair to get it just right, but she was persistent. She tore up two loaves of the previous day's bread into small pieces, then raided the spice cabinet for salt, pepper, celery salt, parsley, and a touch of garlic powder. She liberally spiced the bread, then turned to the cookstove. In a small cast-iron pan, she melted two sticks of butter and chopped up some celery and an onion to simmer in the butter. Then she cracked six brown eggs into the bread and finally added the celery and onion. She used her hands to squish the whole mass together and finished off with a mere drop of milk to make it a bit moister.

She was rinsing her hands at the pump when Joel came in carrying a little white dog. Martha was enchanted. She'd always wanted a dog, but the family had decided that the cost was too high. And they hadn't wanted a part-feral animal.

Now Martha dried her hands on a dishcloth. As she approached, the stray animal leaped playfully into her arms.

"*Ach*, Joel, she's beautiful. May we keep her?"

"Of course. She can both keep you company in the *haus* and learn to herd a bit with me. I don't think she's very *auld* . . . What shall we call her?"

"Sophy," Martha responded promptly.

Joel leaned close to her, reaching to brush a stray tendril of hair from her face. "Have you had that name saved up, sweet Martha?"

"*Jah* . . ." She stood very still, hoping he'd kiss her, but he dropped his hand and moved away.

"Sophy it is. Let's see how she gets along with Puddles."

The gray cat came streaking into the kitchen and skidded to a complete halt as Joel took the dog from Martha's arms and set it on the floor.

Both animals regarded each other warily for a few seconds, then Sophy's plume began to wag and Puddles let out a tender meow.

"Well, that's that." Joel smiled, and Martha nodded.

She felt flustered around him, and became doubly so when he reached in his pants pocket and withdrew a folded sheet of paper.

"Here, sweetheart. I tried to put down some things I've been feeling . . . and, well, you can read it."

"*Nee*. I can't," Martha snapped.

"What?"

She could have bitten her tongue at her brash announcement, but she was tired of having secrets from him. "I can't read, Joel. Your *mamm* has been giving me lessons, but I can't read what you've written here."

"*Ach*, all right." He paused. "I'll read it to you."

"Is that all you're going to say?"

His blue eyes flashed at her. "*Jah*. What's wrong with being a gentleman and reading it for you?"

Martha flounced from the sink, carefully stepping over the two animals. "You could ask me why I cannot read . . . why I cannot write. You could give me a chance to tell my story, or be interested in it. I don't like when you sweep everything under the rug and we don't speak of things. You'd rather just turn the lamps down and *geh* to sleep!"

"What exactly are we talking about here, Martha?"

She hunched a shoulder at him. "Nothing."

She didn't look at him for a long minute, and she finally heard his sigh. "Martha, will you come with me into the bedroom for a minute so we can talk in more privacy?"

"I have the supper to tend to," she muttered, not wanting to *geh* anywhere with him at that moment.

"The stuffing will wait. Please *kumme* . . ."

She hated that she wanted to respond so easily to the husky note in his voice, but he *had* said "please" . . .

# Chapter Twenty-Six

Joel stood in the master bedroom facing his wife, and he had trouble not imagining her in the peach wisp she'd worn for him before. *Men think too much about sex . . . I need to respond to what she said.* "I'm sorry, Martha—I guess I was surprised to learn you can't read, and I just went on with offering to read the note because I didn't want you to think it was a big deal to me."

"Well, it's a big deal to me," she said softly.

Joel sat down on the edge of the bed and patted a spot next to him. "*Kumme* here, will you? And, please, tell me about you and reading and school and anything else that you might want to talk about."

He could see that she was reluctant, but she finally came over and sat down. He reached his arm around her stiff back and pulled her close. "Martha—I love you. Tell me anything you want."

She turned to face him and tears trembled on her lashes. "*Ach,* Joel—you really do love me?"

He stared into the doe-brown depths of her eyes and nodded slowly. "I love you."

Martha swallowed. "Joel, I love you, too, but I've thought—it seems that when we are together . . . making love . . . that you are distant somehow."

Joel took a deep breath, then shook his head. "Martha, I never meant to hurt you. I—I just want to wait a bit until we have children." *Tell her . . . tell her the truth about the vision . . .*

But he could not bring himself to say the words, and a knock on the door interrupted their privacy.

He glanced at Martha, then rose to his feet. "*Kumme* in."

Sophy bounded into the room, and his *mamm* soon followed. "We have a dog, Joel Umble."

"So it would seem, Mamm. Puddles likes her—do you mind?"

Sarah shook her head. "Wouldn't matter much if I did—she's made herself right at home. Are you two bickering?"

Joel had to laugh, and Martha giggled. "*Nee*, Mamm."

"*Gut* . . . because that stuffing won't wait much longer."

Martha got to her feet and reached to kiss Joel's cheek; then she hurried out of the room with Sarah and Sophy on her heels, leaving Joel to think in silence.

Martha turned the bed down carefully, then slipped into a simple cotton shift and started to take the pins out of her hair. Sophy had made herself comfortable at the foot of the bed, with

Puddles in close attendance. Martha thought over the nice supper they'd shared and then, on impulse, took the first letter Joel had given her from the place she'd carefully kept it in the dresser drawer. She opened its folds and went to sit on the side of the bed, trying to puzzle out the sounds of different letters she could now recognize.

Joel entered the room while she was trying to read, and she hastily slid the letter under her hip. She bent her knees and scooted backward on the bed, resting her chin on her kneecaps. She watched her husband undress, sliding his clothes off with unabashed grace, then turning to come to bed. He lay down beside her and rolled onto his side to prop his head up with an elbow. She glanced through veiled lashes at him, studying the tan skin of his arm and the dark thatch of hair at the juncture of his arm and shoulder.

"Will you tell me about your reading?" he asked softly.

"There was always the family to care for . . . they needed me." She shrugged. "I couldn't *geh* to school and we had no money for books or a slate . . . so, that's it."

He reached out to curl a tendril of her hair round his hand. "And you are not bitter."

It was a statement; not a question. "*Nee* . . . I love them. It was my job to honor and care for them."

"I'd like to care for you, Martha Umble."

She felt uncomfortable, restive, under his statement. "I—I don't know how to let someone care for me." It seemed a huge admission, and she let her breath out slowly.

"Can I start by reading the letter that's beneath your charming bottom?"

She felt herself flush, then leaned forward a bit to grasp the letter. She handed it to him.

He opened it slowly, and she tensed. She squeezed her eyes shut tight like a little girl and waited for him to begin.

> My Dearest Martha,
> It is difficult for me to put into words how I feel about you. I also know that reading a "love letter" might not be something you want to do. So, I'll gift you with this poem instead.
>
> "For Martha"
> No gentle fine-boned fawn
> Nor starling on the wing
> No flower cascading humbly
> Can match the words you sing.
>
> A song to win my mind
> With breathless appeal
> You're strong and wondrous
> Gott's child of the field.

You sing of simple joys
The kind to see life through
And there's nothing more I need
Than to spend my life with you.

"It sounds rather silly, I suppose," he ended. "But I mean it."

Martha took the paper from him and pressed it to her breast. "I'll cherish it, Joel Umble, as well as anything else you write and read for me."

She leaned over and pressed her lips warmly to his, falling beside him in the comfortable bed. "Could we practice our lovemaking again?" she asked, emboldened by the warmth of his letter.

She closed her eyes on a sigh when he found the hem of her shift and put his mouth to the crest of her breast.

The next morning dawned bright and fair. It was the second Sunday of the month and time for church service. Joel pulled on a white shirt atop his black pants and glanced at his still-sleeping wife with a tender smile. The *nacht* had been revelatory for both of them; he couldn't help but stop raising his suspenders and fantasizing for a moment but then he ruefully went to wake Martha so they would not be late for the start of service.

# Chapter Twenty-Seven

"And evil begets evil . . . we all know this to be true. If there is evil among us, it must be purged lest we, as a community, begin to suffer." Bishop Loftus paused for a breath, and Martha looked down at the clenched fingers in her lap.

*He means me—I know he does . . .*

She wished she might feel her husband's protective arms around her, but he was seated with all of the other married men, and she with the married women. She tried to distract her thoughts from what was being said by counting the boards in the wall of Deacon Troyer's big barn, but the bishop's voice blasted on.

"If your crops fail, if your children become ill, *jah*, even if your sons die, then you will know that there is a hex or a coven among us. But a witch is clever in her trickery. She may pose as one beleaguered with cares or poverty and then mislead some upstanding man into the devil's ways. *Jah*, she spins a web with her beauty, even her nakedness . . ." Here, Martha saw that the old man paused to lick his lips, and she vowed never to *geh* bathing in the creek again. She drew a shallow breath and kept her head down, idly having the irreverent thought that what was needed here was another strike of lightning . . .

The three-hour-long service dwindled to its close, and only Deacon Troyer's sonorous snoring broke the silence as people got to their feet and began to filter out into the sunlight. It was the first Sunday community dinner to be held outdoors that spring and the youths raced to set up volleyball nets and fetch softballs.

Families had brought quilts or blankets to spread out on the ground, making cozy spots for visiting and eating of the abundant amounts of food.

When Joel met with her on the grassy lawn, Martha handed him the quilt they'd brought. "Here, Joel. If you don't mind, I'm going to walk home and see how Milly and your *mamm* are doing sitting with my family. You stay here and enjoy yourself."

"No, you are not going to listen to that loon Loftus. We'll stay here and have a nice time," Joel said.

"In that case, may I join you?"

Martha turned to see May Miller standing near them, and she smiled. May had somehow ceased to be an imagined rival for her husband's affections and had instead become a friend.

"Of course, May," Martha said gaily.

"And here comes Sebastian." Joel waved his handyman over. "I told him to come for lunch."

Sebastian met May with an easy smile. The

four had just settled on the quilt when Bishop Loftus suddenly loomed up behind them.

"Joel Umble," the older man said in a brusque tone. "What *Englischer* is this who joins our community?"

"My friend, Sebastian. Seb, meet Bishop Loftus."

Martha watched in fascination as an odd expression of aversion crossed the bishop's face. Sebastian had held out a hand in greeting, but the bishop seemed unable to grasp it. It was as if the old man was held bound by something greater than himself. He finally turned with a grunt of dismissal.

"Strange fellow," Sebastian remarked.

"Forget him," Joel muttered, and took Martha's arm. "Let's *geh* taste the food. The tables ought to be near to bowlegged by now. Sebastian, you'll find everything from pickled eggs to raisin pie, and a whole lot in between."

Martha smiled at the handyman. "And try the sherbet punch . . . Joel and I made it together."

She glanced up at her husband and was both pleased and flustered when he bent to kiss her cheek with his warm lips.

Joel tamped down the anger he felt at Bishop Loftus and tried to focus on the scoop of chocolate parfait he'd just piled on his plate. Yet his mood did not improve.

"Ah, don't do it, Joel . . ." Sebastian said from beside him.

"Do what?" Joel was afraid of the answer. Sebastian had an eerie way of pinpointing what a man was thinking.

"Yes, that's right, but don't hang on to your anger, Joel. It eats at a man, makes him bitter and old before his time."

Joel started. "See, that's what I mean—you're enough to scare a body, Sebastian."

"Don't be scared. Just take the advice," Sebastian returned amiably.

Joel nodded. "Maybe I will, at that."

They had just cleaned up and had a rousing match of volleyball when Martha told Joel that she'd be more comfortable going home to check on the folks.

"It's not that I don't think your *mamm* and Milly can manage, but it's the first time I've really been gone, except for when we got married, and—"

"Martha, you don't have to explain." Joel smiled. "It's fine."

Sebastian offered to see May home, and Joel and Martha quickly walked the short distance to the Umble farm. Joel must have caught sight of something on the front porch, though, because Martha suddenly found his lean hand clamped over her eyes.

225

"*Ach*, Martha! It's a surprise. No looking until I say so."

"All right." She let him lead her and caught the enthusiasm emanating from his strong frame.

"Now!" he said.

Martha opened her eyes, completely unprepared for what she saw. Sarah stood just outside the front door, clasping and unclasping her hands as Martha ran up the porch steps after placing a kiss on Sol Kauffman's thinning pate. Milly paced about excitedly. But best of all was seeing the glowing smiles of her *mamm*, *daed*, and *grossmuder* as they sat upright in wheelchairs.

"*Ach*, Joel!" she cried, flying off the porch to throw her arms around her husband's neck. Joel caught her and spun her around clear off the ground.

"It's too much . . . really!"

"Nothing is too much for you and my new family, sweetheart."

She ran back to the porch, talking with each person and thanking *Derr Herr* silently for a husband as thoughtful as Joel.

Later, the family sat in the gloaming together and watched the lightning bugs blink a magical chorus. It was more wonderful than Martha could have imagined.

And after that, when Martha had everyone settled for the night, she slipped out of her dress and shift and took down her hair. Then she hastily crawled beneath the covers before Joel came in. She reached to turn down the lamp to a mellow warmth and sat still, watching Joel undress and admiring his lean frame. When he had everything off, he hurried to the bed, only to discover her own bare skin. They laughed softly together, and he pulled her atop him so that her hair formed a curtain to hide their hot kisses. "You're enchanting," he murmured against her mouth.

"You mean I'm a hex?" she teased, running her short nails down his belly.

"*Jah*," he whispered. "The hex of my heart."

# Chapter Twenty-Eight

The next morning, Martha awoke before dawn, only to find Joel already gone from the bed. She dressed hurriedly, wondering at the hole in the window, and went out to the kitchen.

Joel was busily scrambling eggs, and she stretched up on her tiptoes to kiss his cheek. "Why are you up so early?" she murmured, not wanting to break the peacefulness of the dawn.

"I was hoping to make you breakfast in bed, but since you're up—we can share."

She sat down at the table at his invitation. Then he fed her hotcakes and raspberry jam with his lean fingertips, pausing to give her sweet, sticky kisses that made her hungry for more. He allowed her a fork for her eggs but took it back to give her bites of bacon.

"Joel?"

"Hmmm?"

"What happened to the bedroom window? I remember something from the *nacht*, but I thought I was dreaming."

He shrugged and moved closer to kiss jam from the edge of her mouth. "A night bird, sweetheart. Too focused on the hunt. There's nothing to worry about. I'll get some glass from Sol when he opens."

She looped her arms around his shoulders. "Why do I think there's something you're not telling me?"

He kissed her deeply and gave a deep-throated laugh. "Let's concentrate on the raspberry jam . . . I never knew it could be so . . . rich and thick."

Martha had to agree, but something niggled at the back of her consciousness that went beyond the sweet kisses they shared.

Joel knew it was wrong to lie to Martha, but he couldn't bring himself to worry her. He threw the piece of coal up and caught it as he walked to Sol's, finally tossing it away in the brush.

Little Jacob Mast stepped out onto the path in front of him. "Hey, Jacob, how have you been?" Joel asked.

"Pretty *gut*. You still kissin' girls?"

Joel laughed. "Sometimes. You know I haven't seen you since the day Sebastian brought you back."

"*Ach* . . . him. He's an angel."

Joel ruffled the child's hair. "Is that what your *mamm* says?"

Jacob wrinkled his nose. "*Nee*."

"Then why call Sebastian an angel?"

"I was dead for a while and he was all white and shiny and when he picked me up—I came back to life."

Joel blinked. "Okaaay. But I think you were just imagining that—"

"No. That's playing with your mind. This wasn't playing, and I know he's an angel. Maybe he's here to help you too. Okay. Gotta go. See ya!"

Joel watched the child disappear around a bend in the path and shook his head. *One of these days, I need to have a talk with my hired man . . .*

That evening, after a filling supper, Joel went out on the front porch alone to stare up at the stars, his thoughts running in a thousand directions. But he was mostly focused on his wife and the smile of love she'd shown him the day before when she'd seen her family in their wheelchairs, suddenly having the ability to move again.

He dragged his thoughts back to the present when he heard the screen door open and then slam again and turned to see his father-in-law trying to make it out onto the porch in his wheelchair. Joel moved to help him, but Chet Yoder waved him off with a frustrated grunt.

"No, *buwe*. Let me try."

It was frustrating to watch someone struggle, but Joel recognized the importance of the other man's independence and his need to be self-reliant after so many years of enforced care.

Chet finally made it through the door and wheeled himself out onto the porch, gasping a bit for breath. Joel let him compose himself and then remarked on the stars.

"The *nacht* sky always settles me somehow."

"Used to calm me too," Chet muttered.

"And now it doesn't?" Joel felt like he should tread lightly with this man he hardly knew but respected deeply as Martha's *fater*.

"*Nee*, not much can bring me calm now, though I'm grateful for this chair . . . *Ach*, I miss working, especially with my hands . . . Makes a man feel useless when he can't work."

Joel felt a sudden idea form in his head. "Chet, do you think you'd like one of the smaller barns to be made into a workshop for you? There's a lot of things we could set up for—like fine woodworking or leather work . . ."

"How would I get there? I can't run this thing through mud and such."

"Sebastian and I could make a wooden walkway for you and then build shelves and things at a low level so you could reach them easily . . . What do you say?"

Joel waited.

Chet's voice rasped when it came. "I'd be mighty thankful, *sohn* . . . I'd be blessed."

Joel nodded and swallowed. "We'll get it done soon."

"*Danki, buwe.*"

The two men said nothing more, but relaxed in the rich blanket of *nacht* that spread itself over the mountain.

Martha's strong arms easily pushed her *mamm*'s wheelchair down to the area allotted for the kitchen garden.

"*Ach*, Martha, it's been so long since I've been able to see a garden. It does my soul *gut*! You must tell me, child, what everything is, since it's just beginning."

Martha bent to kiss her *mamm*'s cheek and then began to point to various specks of green that showed promise against the rich earth.

"Bush beans, eggplant, muskmelon, kidney beans, Swiss chard, turnips, potatoes, and watermelon—just to name a few!"

"*Wunderbarr*!" Her *mamm*'s gentle hands clapped lightly, as if she'd just seen a performance of the highest art.

"Is your asthma all right out here?" Martha asked, returning to the chair.

"*Ach, jah*—I haven't felt so good in a long while, but now I insist that you take me back. If you can manage with Milly to bring your father and then *grossmuder* out . . ."

"All right, Mamm."

Martha turned the chair back toward the *haus* and found herself humming with pleasure.

• • •

Joel replaced the glass in the master bedroom window with a minimum of fuss, then went outside to look for Sebastian.

Jacob Mast's claims about Seb sort of hovered at the back of Joel's mind. The *Englischer* did have an uncanny insight into things . . .

Sebastian was sitting on the creek bank on a comfortable-looking bed of moss, bottle-feeding one of the lambs that had been rejected by an older ewe.

Joel sat down and stared out into the rush of the creek.

"Something on your mind, boss?" Seb asked easily.

Joel looked at him out of the corner of his eye. "Are you an angel, Seb?"

The sound of the lamb guzzling took hold of Joel's mind, and he decided he was being distinctly foolish.

"Well, Joel, who told you that I'm an angel?"

"Jacob Mast."

"Uh-huh. Well, I suppose the answer would be yes—I'm an angel, but I think I make a rather good hired hand too."

Joel nodded, not missing a beat. "Yep. You are at that, Seb. You truly are."

# Chapter Twenty-Nine

The following day, May Miller stopped by in the afternoon and Martha was glad to offer her teaberry tea and the first piece of an angel food cake.

The two sat down together afterward on the porch swing and May talked about some new medicine tinctures she wanted to try for Martha's *mamm*'s asthma now that she had improved.

May also brought word of a painting frolic that was coming up.

"Frau Raber is having her front room brightened up, so she and those two girls of hers have turned it into a frolic."

"I've never been to a frolic," Martha said worriedly. "What do we do?"

May smiled. "You paint, eat, and gossip, though I usually leave early. The menfolk go and get drunk with Sol Kauffman, passing around the jug of moonshine."

"*Ach* . . ." Martha said softly, not knowing if she liked the idea of Joel drinking.

"Joel won't drink much, if at all," May said comfortably.

"You know him so well, don't you? Sometimes I feel—well, at a loss as to what he's really thinking."

"Why not ask him?" May suggested with her usual practicality, but Martha shook her head. "He puts me off . . . like when we were at the Ice Mine together and he—well, he saw something but wouldn't talk about it."

"Sometimes, the second sight is not always a gift."

"You have it, too, don't you?"

May shrugged. "I suppose so. It helps in being a healer."

Martha nodded. "I would think so."

"We each have our gifts from *Gott*, Martha, and your gifts captured Joel's heart."

*More like my body captured him,* Martha thought, then berated herself silently for such negative thinking.

"Has Joel—well, ever said he doesn't like *kinner*?" Martha asked with a frown between her brows.

"Joel? I don't think so. Why do you ask?"

Martha was saved from a reply by Joel's arrival from the sheep barn. He smiled at May, then bent to kiss Martha. She loved the manly smell of him—both sweat and sunshine, all mixed together in a way that made her feel positively addled.

"I'm going to get some spring water from Bury Hollow—your *grossmuder* was thirsting for some last *nacht*."

"*Ach, danki*, Joel."

May got to her feet and made for the screen door of the house. "You two *geh* on and have a nice walk. I'll stay here for a while."

Martha decided to take her new friend up on her offer and hurried to smooth the sleeves of her light blue dress while Joel fetched two glass jugs to put the water in.

They set out at a brisk pace, and Martha wondered if he was even paying attention to how much ground he was covering while she had to practically run to keep up. *Men,* she thought ruefully, then smiled that he was hers.

"I'm sorry, Martha, for hurrying so. I guess I was thinking too much."

"I'm fine," she said airily, then nearly stumbled, so that he slung a warm arm around her waist while Sophy jumped and frisked around them.

They got to the aptly named Bury Hollow and sought out the spring. The hollow was cool even on the hottest days, and shadows played with mountain rosebushes, turning their leaves and thorns dark. But the spring water was some of the most refreshing to be found on the mountain, and Joel offered Martha the tin dipper that hung on a branch near the spring.

He watched her as she drank—the pouty fullness of her lips and then the play of water down her throat as she worked to drink deep. She turned to hand him the dipper, and he shook his

236

head. "Fill up your hands, sweet wife. I'd rather drink from your fingers."

He watched her color delightfully, then lean forward to let the water cascade over her cupped hands. She hurried to raise it to his lips, and he accepted the brief sips she could hold. She did it again, and this time he slid a finger between her apron and her dress, toying with the fabric.

"You look pretty in blue."

"*Danki*," she said primly, stretching to hang the dipper back on the branch. He caught her close on her descent, turning her so that her back was against his chest. He ran questing hands down her supple figure, taking in her clean scent and enticing warmth.

"Mmmm," he murmured in appreciation. "But far too many layers, I'm afraid."

She giggled and turned to face him, stretching to kiss his mouth and then tease his lips with her tongue. But he gave as good as she until there was no help for it but to either seek the damp earth or go home to find pleasure in their own bed.

"*Kumme*, love, let's find out if we can sneak in an afternoon—nap—without being noticed."

"You know that it will be noticed."

"Maybe everyone will be too busy drinking spring water to give it a second thought," he teased, flicking at her *kapp* string, then catching her close for one more heated kiss . . .

# Chapter Thirty

The morning of the paint frolic was upon her before she noticed, and Martha found herself flustered and only half-ready when it was time to *geh*.

"Don't worry," Joel said softly to her as she threw plain simplicity out the window and coiled her hair for the third time.

"It's easy for you to say not to worry—all you have to do is drink . . . Maybe I should *geh* with you," she said, giggling.

"And all you have to do is paint, eat, and *kumme* home."

"You've forgotten the gossip, Joel . . . what about that? Didn't I hear from your *mamm* that Ruby Raber was sweet on you before we married? Suppose she wants to discuss old times?"

"Ignore her and have fun with May. All right, I'll see you this afternoon." He bent and kissed her briefly and she hurried to finish dressing. She left an unhappy Sophy behind, but Sarah and Milly promised to keep an eye on the little dog, and on everyone else too.

She arrived at the Rabers' and heard a cheerful crowd already gathered inside—which did nothing to help her nervousness. But when she knocked, Frau Raber opened the door and swept her inside. Martha saw May painting some white trim by the stair steps and hurried to join her.

"I'm so glad you're here," Martha confided, grabbing a small paintbrush and concentrating diligently on one small space, hoping she could make it last for an hour.

Joel entered the back of Sol Kauffman's store through the side door he saw other fellas going through. He was prepared for the usual scent of moonshine but hadn't expected it so early in the morning.

"*Ach*, Joel Umble. *Kumme* in. I just got some fresh oranges sent up from down Coudersport way. You *kumme* on and have some moonshine and orange juice—it'll do ya *gut*!"

The recipe didn't sound entirely unappealing, so he had a glass, then ate some biscuits and honey. By the time he'd had his fourth glass, he couldn't quite see straight and he had an aching desire to spend a few private hours with his wife.

He decided to stop by the paint frolic on his way home and had to endure a lot of groaning on the part of his friends when he slurred that he was newly married and that he missed Martha.

But he couldn't seem to remember the direction to the Raber *haus* and decided that home sounded better anyway. When he got there, he sat on the front steps trying to cool the bad headache he felt coming on and was grateful for Sebastian's strong arm and lack of comment as he saw him off to bed. He drifted close to sleep but not before he remembered Martha and wished she was having as good a time as he certainly had not . . .

Martha took a bite of the chilled pea salad and decided it needed salt—not that she'd ever had chilled pea salad, but she thought it would benefit from some pepper as well. She stayed mostly quiet while the other women talked and gossiped, glad to sit in May's shadow.

She balanced her plate on her knees and looked around at the newly painted light blue room. It did look well, and Martha felt a sense of satisfaction that she could help her neighbors.

May had gone to get some punch, and Martha was unprepared for Ruby Raber to take the vacant seat. Martha smiled and nodded, hoping the other girl wouldn't mention Joel.

"I suppose it's only going to be a matter of time until you're fat with child."

Martha arched an eyebrow and tried to push aside the fact that the room had grown quieter, and her heart hurt a bit from the cruel remark and Joel's seeming desire to not have her fat with child.

Still, Ruby Raber opened her mouth to fire off another insult, and Martha shook her head as if addressing an errant child. "Don't."

"Don't what, Martha Married for Money Umble?"

Martha sighed and rose to her feet. She calmly dumped the unsalted pea salad onto Ruby Raber's head, ignoring the other girl's shrieks of rage.

Martha thanked her bemused hostess, waved to May, and quickly walked home. If they hadn't thought her a hex before, she now had removed all doubt.

Joel came awake in slow degrees. He was aware that Martha was moving quietly about the room, and he tried to sit up, but found that the room spun and his head throbbed.

"Sebastian said you'd had too much orange juice. Are you feeling lousy?" Martha's voice was barely above a whisper, but the sound hurt just the same.

"What time is it?"

"Two in the afternoon."

"What? Wait—why are you home so early?"

"Bad pea salad."

He nodded without understanding and reached up a hand for her to hold. "I missed you," he whispered.

She sat down carefully on the bed beside him. "*Ach*, Joel, and I missed you. I think I'm someone who likes to be at home—providing that you're here, of course."

Her innocent admission touched his heart, and he pulled her down to rest her head on his chest.

# Chapter Thirty-One

The next morning, Martha was hanging out sheets on the clothesline. She loved to feel them billow, damp and sweet-smelling, against her, and she loved even more when the mountain breezes puffed them up like substantial pregnant bellies. She shook her head and muttered to herself, "I've got *bopplis* on the brain."

Joel and Sebastian were weeding the garden, and she had just taken off her shoes to *geh* and help them when she noticed Sol Kauffman break the tree line to hurry over to Joel. The older man was gone even before she could hear what was said, but she raised a questioning and interested brow at Joel.

"Deacon Troyer passed away last *nacht* in his sleep."

"*Ach*, his poor wife," Martha murmured, already thumbing through the kitchen's recipe books mentally to think what she might take the grieving widow.

"The man slept so much, I'm not sure how long it's been since he actually performed the duties of deacon," Joel commented.

"I can't even remember having another deacon. He was deacon so long, I guess I'm not sure what he was supposed to be doing," Martha said aloud.

Sebastian heard her and paused in his hoeing. "A deacon is to be the servant of the poor—that is, in Amish culture."

Joel nodded. "*Jah*, either the literally poor or those who are struggling and poor in spirit."

"Then it's a serious job," Martha said. "And there is no pay and it's to last a lifetime, right?" she asked.

Joel nodded. "Yes, for a lifetime, unless the deacon were to become bishop, which almost never happens."

"Why not?"

"Because most deacons are too young, don't have the right experience and so on."

"*Ach*, well," Martha murmured, picking up a hoe, "*Gott* will decide, I suppose."

Martha was surprised when Sebastian smiled at her with warmth and nodded. "Indeed He will!"


Joel was unprepared for the rush of fervor that took over the community after Deacon Troyer was buried. There was constant speculation as to who should be chosen by lot to serve as the new deacon.

"I feel sorry for whoever it is," Joel confided one *nacht* to Martha in bed. "That man is going to have to deal with Loftus for a long time."

"Let's talk of something else," Martha suggested, leaning over to run her fingers through the light mat of hair on his chest. Joel was only too willing to oblige.

The next day was the spring communion church service—the only time a new deacon might be chosen. Martha sat with the other married women until it was time to whisper through a crack in a closet door and tell the bishop whom she thought should be nominated for deacon. Bishop Loftus would then make tallies and see which men were to draw lots to become the servant of the poor.

It was a lengthy process, but in the end, Martha waited anxiously to see what names would be called.

"Solomon Kauffman," the bishop intoned. "Abner Mast." And here the bishop gave an audible sigh. "Joel Umble."

Martha wanted to clap, although she knew that others around her were actually mourning. To be chosen as deacon was a solemn affair, and it meant that the man would have twice the usual amount of work for the rest of his life.

Martha watched as the three men filed forward. Then they sat down on the front row of the benches. Bishop Loftus brought forth three hymnals—one for each man to choose. In one of the hymnals was a slip of paper with a Bible verse written on it. The man who chose that hymnal would be ordained as deacon.

Martha waited as each of the three chose a hymnal from the bishop's hands, and she prayed that Joel would choose the one that best pleased *Derr Herr*.

Joel sat holding the hymnal, wondering who in the world would have nominated him. *I'm young, half-crazed with longing at times for my wife, I keep secrets from Martha, and I—*

"Joel Umble," the bishop snapped. "Will you open your hymnal?"

Joel looked up into the man's eyes. Yep, definitely shark eyes . . .

Joel flipped open the hymnal, and the slip of paper fluttered out. He caught it before it reached the floor. He felt Sol Kauffman relax next to him at not having been chosen.

"Joel Umble," the bishop said. "You will read the verse on the slip of paper aloud to the community to begin your ordination."

Joel wanted to sigh, but he got to his feet and opened the paper, staring down at it in disbelief. *"Thou shalt not suffer a witch to live . . ."*

Suddenly rage and clarity flooded his mind at the same time. He lifted his chin and straightened his spine. "The verse reads . . . 'God is love.' " He turned and sat down, knowing he had no further part to play in the service but having no doubt he'd have to deal with Loftus later. It was not an encouraging thought . . .

# Chapter Thirty-Two

Spring wound around to the time for the community mud sales. These were the Ice Mountain equivalent of a suburban town's yard sales, and Martha was excited. She remembered long ago going with her *daed* to a mud sale where she'd found a small stuffed dog for a nickel. Her father had bought it for her, and she had treasured it. That little stuffed animal had been her companion for many a long *nacht* when the day had seemed too hard. But today, she needed to ask Sarah if there was anything she might like to sell.

"*Geh* up to the attic and take what you want, Martha—except my kneading bowls and archery equipment, *ach*, and the bowling pins—not the birdcage, either, though I do hate to see a bird caged . . . *Jah*, that's it."

Martha nodded, her mind whirling. She made her way up to the dusty attic and gazed around with interest and pleasure at the many old-fashioned trunks that dotted the floor space. She bypassed the bow and arrows and went to kneel beside an *auld* walnut chest. When she lifted the lid, the odor of cedar came to her, and she breathed in appreciatively. Then she removed a layer of tissue paper and opened her mouth in a soft "O" of pleasure. Tiny boys' baby clothes filled the trunk with even more incredibly small black shoes with solid, rounded soles.

She brought a blanket to her cheek and knew that she wanted a *haus*ful of *kinner* to love and cherish with Joel.

"What do you have there?" Joel asked, raising a lantern and coming over to her. He sat down on the floor next to her and looped one long finger in the laces of a shoe. "My *boppli* stuff, I think. I didn't know that Mamm had kept it all."

"It's lovely," she whispered, longing to talk to him about the way she felt.

"It's a good cedar-lined trunk—it keeps the mice away."

Martha nodded, then took a deep breath. "Joel, I know it's only been a short while since we married, but I wondered if you'd had any time to maybe change your mind about a *boppli*? I mean—I'll wait, but . . ."

He dropped the shoe and pressed his hand over hers. "Martha, sweet Martha, it's not that easy. I want it to be, though—I want to hold you and make love to you and not have to always stop . . . But . . ." She watched him lower his head.

"What is it, Joel?"

She saw his throat work, and then he looked at her, his eyes near navy blue and his pupils dilated.

"Martha, I had a vision at the Ice Mine—I saw—I saw you laboring to bring forth a babe, and you were screaming . . ."

She felt his hand tighten on hers. "Martha, the baby died. There were seven tombstones in the vision—one for each of our children. Martha, they all died. I decided then and there that I will not put you through that."

She bowed her head for a moment, then looked back into his eyes with a steady surety. "Joel—your vision—it could be wrong or it could change. We don't know what *Gott* has willed or planned for us, but I do know that I love you and love can bear all things."

"Martha, I love you too. And—I guess I forgot for a while that I'm not in charge of our future. Having you, having us strong together . . . *Ach*, Martha . . . you're right. We can bear all things together in *Gott*'s grace."

She smiled at him through happy tears and asked one more question. "Was there an eighth stone?"

He stared at her blankly. "An eighth stone? What?"

She leaned forward and pressed her forehead to his. "Joel, I'd carry your children seven times, even if meant that we only got to love them here for a little while—they'd be part of you, of us. And . . . well, I expect I would scream in childbirth—women do, you know. But Joel, dear sweet wonderful Joel—there was no eighth stone. It's something to rejoice in!"

She watched him shake his head, and then he pulled her close and put his mouth against her throat, trying to get closer. "Martha Umble, you are the bravest person I've ever met, and I am honored to be by your side in this life."

She squeezed him back and felt happy tears fill her eyes. "I love you, Joel Umble, and always will." She looked at him from beneath damp lashes, and a smile played about her full lips.

"What is it?" he asked.

"We could start making babies right now . . . right here."

He smiled slowly, a flash of white teeth in the half darkness. And then he swept her to the floor beside him. "Making babies, hmm? I promise to give it my—utmost attention."

"And how will you do that?" Martha asked coyly.

"*Ach*, with peach *nacht* shifts and delicious blue garters—I want you to wear those for me tonight."

She laughed in delight at the command. "I will gladly do as you ask—but only if you wear what I ask . . ."

"Anything," he muttered as he freed her hair from its pins.

"Actually, I was thinking nothing. You'll wear nothing."

"I can do that," he whispered. "If you help me, I can do that right now."

She sat up and ran her fingers beneath his suspenders, feeling the rapid rise and fall of his chest beneath his blue shirt. "You'll have to sit up, Herr Umble, if you please."

"Right."

He sat up slowly, as if he were dazed, and Martha rejoiced inside at his arousal.

He kept his hands on her while she eased his suspenders down. Then she found the pins to his shirtfront and flung them away with little patters of sound.

She shivered deliciously as she ran her hands over his chest and down to the leanness of his ribs. He helped her get his shirt off as she paused to take quick nips across his chest.

"I owe you for that," he rasped.

She swallowed hard, her own skin tingling beneath the weight of her dress and apron. Then she forced herself to concentrate and ordered him to stand up.

"I can't," he half laughed. "I can't stop kissing you."

"Try," she choked as he sucked hard at the juncture of her neck and shoulder.

He finally got to his feet, and she knelt upward so that she was level with the dark, arrowed hair of his belly.

"Hurry, please . . ." he begged, and she

took a fierce grip on her own emotions.

"Boots first," she reminded him, as if she were his teacher.

He bent and helped her with the laces, his breathing fast and shallow, and she had his boots and socks off in seconds. Now he stood again, his head back a bit, his eyes closed as he caught the sides of her face in his hands and held her close to him. She ran her fingers inside the waistband of his black pants at his hips, teasingly letting her hands move forward and back.

"Dear *Gott*, Martha . . . I can't . . . I want . . ."

"I know," she said soothingly, then helped him ease the pants off until he stood naked before her. She let herself touch him everywhere but the rampant part of him that taunted and pressed against the flesh of his belly.

Then he dropped back to the floor beside her. "I can't wait much longer," he confessed and started to reach through the layers of her clothes.

"You don't have to wait, Joel."

He made love to her while she was still dressed, and the luxuriant feel of his smooth skin against the rasp of her clothing was enough to make her gasp for air as he pushed hard and whispered small words of encouragement to her. She soon dissolved in a thousand grains of spun sugar and then knew he'd had his own pleasure by the sobbing breaths he drew and the way he held her close. No trying to stop a *boppli* this time, she thought in dazed pleasure. No stopping at all . . .

Much later, Seb hailed Joel as he headed for the sheep barn. "Hey, boss, wondered if you'd like to take a walk with me up to the high timber."

Joel stopped still. "You're leaving, aren't you?"

Seb nodded cheerfully. "I am but a servant as you are, Deacon Umble. It is time for me to go."

Joel swallowed. "Will I see you again in this—lifetime?"

"Hard to tell." Sebastian extended a hand, and Joel shook it heartily. He knew that Seb's leaving was necessary somehow, and he turned to fall into step with him as they started the climb to the high timber.

"Hey, Seb?"

"Mmm-hmm?"

"Was young Jacob Mast dead when you found him?"

Seb smiled. "I think we're all a little bit dead until we find hope and friendship and love."

And Joel knew that these were words to base a lifetime upon.

"And you truly are . . . ?" Joel asked, trying to grasp what seemed impossible. "But why me?" Sebastian looked out at the flock of sheep. "Angels are messengers or servants or protectors . . . At times lately, you've seemed to need all of these."

Joel half laughed. "You're right about that, but really—so many people need protectors. Why me?"

Sebastian spoke meditatively. "Someday, a great many people will need you, Joel. Need you to serve them and speak for them and protect them. I'm here to help you get going on that path.

"And my kind are always around. Always fighting against the—opposition, you might say."

"You mean evil, don't you?"

Seb nodded. "Yep."

Joel spoke slowly. "I never understood my brother . . . Judah was—he seemed evil to me, though I hate to speak of him like that . . . He was my older *bruder* and I wanted to love him . . . He never let me."

"No, he was a difficult case, and he fell under the wrong influence . . . But some people are like that, Joel. They resist love, authentic love. They might be hurt themselves or simply making a choice. But love has no place in their lives . . . And oh, I'm not talking about some romanticized love . . . No, I mean the love that is action and doing and giving—wholehearted, sold-out, and sacrificing for others."

Joel looked at him and felt as if he were being swallowed up by those gentle eyes. "You will love like that, Joel. You will lead like that. And . . . well, I suppose that I've said too much . . .

My time here is about done. It's time for me to go on alone from here."

"All right. Hey, Seb . . . ?"

"Yes?"

Joel wiped the tears from his eyes and spoke softly. "Thank you."

# Chapter Thirty-Three

Martha bent over the tiny kitchen garden plants that were growing stronger each day and then paused to watch Sophy unsuccessfully chase chipmunks. She felt a peacefulness in her soul, as if her days were now strung together like drops of pearl and that she was truly blessed.

She was surprised when Sophy's normally cheerful bark turned to a fierce growling. Martha looked up to see Bishop Loftus walking toward her with a determined gait, totally ignoring the dog. Martha swallowed and gripped the hoe she held as if she might have to defend herself. But then she told herself that it was the bright light of day and she was only a call away from the *haus*.

Martha set her lips and managed a polite greeting when the man came to stand less than two rows away from her in the garden. "Hello, Bishop Loftus."

"Your hair is coming down," he practically growled, and Martha hastily put her hand to the loose tendrils that had worked their way from her *kapp* while she worked.

"I—I shall *geh* and fix it now." It was, she thought, the perfect reason to escape the man's presence.

"*Nee*," he said. "I have come here to risk speaking with you."

"Risk?" she questioned.

"You are a hex, and I take great risk to my soul in addressing you, but you have been a thorn in my flesh long enough."

She stared at him, wondering how he had gotten so odd in the head.

"I have been having trouble with my eyesight of late, and I know it is you who has put this curse upon me."

Martha had no words, but she tried to be reasonable. "I could not and did not curse you."

"Liar!" he hissed. "I saw you in your cauldron, seducing an innocent man who was fool enough to marry you. You're a witch! And your baser nature was revealed as your body was bared. No doubt that was the moment my eyes were cursed."

Martha gasped. "You watched Joel and me in the creek? You watched me bathing? You're a twisted and sinful man, and I will tell my—"

"You will tell no one." He took a step closer to her, and she tightened her grip on the hoe even further. "And you will tempt me no further to sin or I will see you stripped naked and horsewhipped, as should be done to beat the evil from you."

Martha noticed that his dark eyes glittered, and he wet his lips. She was repulsed and thought of

Judah and his preoccupation with beating her sin from her, his excitement when he was hurting her. The bishop was voicing the same ideas, and she wondered if he'd been behind Judah's obsession all along. She stood mesmerized, as if gazing into the eyes of a big snake.

The bishop seemed to note her paralysis and took advantage to step near her and to boldly pinch her breast.

Martha reacted without thought and brought the handle of the hoe down hard on the man's head. "Who do you think you are?" she cried, pushing past him to run to the sheep barn, where she knew Joel was working. She didn't stop to look back.

Joel looked up from the ewe he was tending to see his wife come bursting into the barn, sobbing as she ran. "Joel, *ach*, Joel!"

He caught her against him and felt the rapid beating of her heart.

"He grabbed my breast . . . *Ach*, I think I'm going to be sick." She sagged to her knees in the straw, and Joel followed her.

"Who? Martha, you must tell me what you're talking about. Just calm down."

Joel caught her wild-eyed look, and she seemed to steady herself while gazing into his eyes.

"The bishop . . . he came to the garden and he called me a hex and grabbed me. He saw me naked in the creek and watched us . . . *Ach*, Joel!"

Joel pulled her close and gently stroked her back. "It's all right, Martha. It's all right. Are you hurt anywhere? Did he hurt you?"

She shook her head. "*Nee*, but I was scared and angry, Joel. I—I hit him with the hoe."

Joel smiled. "Well done, my love! Now let me *geh* out and finish what's left after the hoe."

But Martha caught him by his arms. "*Nee*, Joel, *sei se gut*, let him be."

"Why would I do that? Dear *Gott*—he's as bad as Judah was."

"I'm all right, Joel. I—I want to let *Gott* handle this. I do not want to cause any trouble in the community."

"Trouble in the—*nee*, I—" He broke off suddenly and leaned forward to try to rest his head on her shoulder. It was another vision that had taken him right when his wife needed him most. He tried to break away from it, but the vision held—enlarging, clearing, until he saw that he stood next to Bishop Loftus's bed and the room was dimly lit. The old man seemed to be gasping for breath, and clutched his chest as if in great pain. Blood ran from his nose and he turned his head. His eyes seemed to lock with Joel's, to plead, but then there was nothing and Joel was back in the barn, holding Martha close again.

"Joel? Are you all right? Did you have another vision?"

He nodded slowly. "It was Loftus—he was—I think he was dying . . ."

"*Ach*, Joel, you must let this *geh* as I've told you. You cannot be responsible for killing a man."

Joel smiled sadly. "I didn't hurt him—he lay in his bed. His eyes—his eyes reminded me of Judah . . ."

Martha swiped at the tears on her cheeks. "We will say nothing of what happened today—*Gott* will handle it. I know He will. Please, Joel, promise me that you won't see Bishop Loftus or try to get even with him . . ."

"I promise. I promise because I think his time is short and I—I think I'm supposed to tell him that, Martha. I think his eyes looked at me—I don't know. I sound *narrish*."

He clung to her for a moment, then gently kissed her lips. "We will see what comes to pass."

# Chapter Thirty-Four

The fullness of spring had brought its rich beauty to the mountain when Martha heard for the first time about the spring program that the *kinner* would be putting on at school.

She was arranging pussy willows in a deep jar when Joel looped an arm around her waist and pulled her close. "Don't forget, my love, that this Saturday is the school program."

She turned in his arms and stretched to kiss his tanned throat. "What school program is that?"

"*Ach* . . . I'm sorry, Martha. I thought you knew. There's a spring program that the kids have every year to raise money for new books . . . I'd be honored to take you if you want to *geh*?"

She smiled widely. "Of course I want to go. My own reading lessons with your *mamm* have been going really well, and since I didn't *geh* to school myself, I've never been to a spring program. It'll be educational!"

He laughed and bent to hug her closer, and she rejoiced simply to be in his arms.

Joel put the last board in place and nailed it down firm.

He then walked over everything to make sure it was secure. It had taken him some time to complete and transform one of the smaller barns into a workshop for his father-in-law. But now it was finished, and the walkway between *haus* and barn was complete as well. He walked back to the porch and went in to find Chet working a puzzle of blue jays near the living area's large window.

The older man's big hands seemed to struggle to maneuver the small pieces, and Joel felt good inside knowing that the new shop would give Chet something more engaging to do.

"It's finished," Joel announced, and Chet rolled his chair back from the table with a sigh of relief.

"*Danki, buwe.* I'm just about over trying to work puzzles and such."

"Well, you won't have to anymore. May I take you outside?"

Joel carefully navigated the chair onto the front porch, then gestured to the ramp and wooden walkway. "Please . . . after you."

Chet gave him a grin, then eased the chair down the ramp, only to gather speed on the wide wooden planks.

Joel followed and then waited as Chet grasped the low-placed handle and slid the workshop door open wide.

"I hope you like it," Joel said softly. He watched as the older man slowly moved forward, drinking in each detail.

Joel had taken care to make the shelves at just the right height and had bought a fine set of tools from Sol Kauffman.

Chet picked up a screwdriver, and his big hand shook. "Too much, *buwe*. You did too much."

"You are my *fater* and have blessed my life with your beautiful daughter. I could never do too much for you."

Joel stepped forward and put a hand on Chet's shoulder, only to have it grasped tightly by the other man. It was a moving feeling, and Joel knew a sense of completeness in his soul.

The Saturday of the spring program dawned bright and clear. Martha took care with her dress, pulling on the fabric of a subtle pumpkin color that brought out the shine of her hair and eyes. And Joel noticed.

He caught her around the waist when she would have put her apron on. "Joel, we have to get ready to *geh*. Now behave," she playfully implored.

"Mmmm, I'll behave . . . exactly the way you need . . . It'll be no trouble to slip off that delicious dress—I promise."

His hands were already matching his words, quickly lifting the dress over her head and laying it neatly on the bottom of the bed. He kept his promise despite her faint protests, which quickly turned into soft cries of heated pleasure.

• • •

They were only a bit late to the program, and Joel felt it well worth the struggle to find seats when he could still see the flush of passion on Martha's cheeks.

He sat next to her and automatically took her hand in his as Bishop Loftus rose to make opening remarks.

He knew that Martha had tried to forget what the man had said and done to her, but it was not easy. But then Joel murmured in her ear, soft words describing how he'd felt less than half an hour before, and he knew she didn't even notice when the bishop had finished speaking and taken a seat.

Joel had to admit to himself that the teacher, Tabby Stolfus, who was Milly's *mamm*, had done an excellent job preparing the *kinner* to sing and recite. They were sweetly off-key, but Joel loved it all the same.

As he sat, he let his eyes drift over the crowd, thinking about the things that Sebastian had told him. He wondered for the umpteenth time what the angel had meant by Joel leading and then dismissed the thought as he looked at Martha and saw her genuine pleasure in the children and their accomplishments.

Martha had felt a sourness in her stomach when the bishop had risen to speak, but she had quickly forgotten the *aulder* man when Joel teased gently in her ear.

But now she rejoiced in the children's reading—following along in her mind with the younger class's recitations and loving the simple poems that were read as a welcome to spring.

After the program, she and Joel walked slowly home, taking their time, stopping to kiss and kiss again, until she felt as though she sipped fine dandelion wine as she reveled in how much she loved and desired her husband.

# Chapter Thirty-Five

There was a fine, misting rain dampening the mountain day, and Martha decided to clean off the back porch, which was a catchall for boots, shoes, fishing gear, and the odd box or so.

Martha found one cardboard box that held a variety of books, and she carried it inside the *haus*, thinking the books were probably Joel's. But when she set the box on the kitchen table, she had the strange urge to look through the books, rejoicing in the fact that she could now read most of the titles.

She glanced through the covers, not sure what she sought, but seeking all the same.

Joel came whistling into the kitchen, and she looked up just as her hand brushed the leather spine of a book. It was slender, easily lost between two bigger novels. She took the leather-covered book from the box and examined it more closely. With newfound confidence she opened the cover, finally able to make sense of the words written inside. But what she read there almost caused her to drop the slim volume before she handed it to Joel.

"It may sound strange, but I think that's Judah's journal." She waited expectantly until Joel opened it.

265

She watched him skim the inside cover and then he smiled at her. "It is. It's Judah's."

He bent and kissed her. "*Danki*, sweetheart."

"You're welcome . . . but I have no idea how it got here."

Joel shook his dark head. "Actually, I got the books from a pile Bishop Loftus had. He was trying to figure out which ones were appropriate for the school *kinner*. I grabbed a handful or two of the others he wanted to give away."

Joel was skimming pages and stopped suddenly. "Listen to this," Joel choked out. " 'Today I shot Dan Zook as he lay asleep in his bed. It was hard at first to take a life, but I did it to please my master, to show my worth. *Auld* Dan will *geh* to heaven anyway, so what does it matter?' "

Martha put her arms around him. "*Ach*, Joel. I'm so sorry. How awful to know that Judah committed such a crime. And Dan was your friend too."

Joel drew a deep breath. "Notice how he says 'his master.' I know he doesn't mean *Gott*. It's Loftus—they were two of a kind, or else maybe Judah was simply mesmerized by the man. You know, evil calls and some answer. Just think about what Adolf Hitler was able to make people choose to do."

Martha continued to keep her arms around him as he slowly worked through his thoughts.

Painfully, he continued to read aloud, the words on each page seeming to leap at them with venomous hatred. When Joel finally stopped, there was a long silence.

"Stephen Lambert was shunned because of a lie—there have been so many lies and half-truths. Always victimizing those who have the least power to fight back," Joel said slowly. "I am going to pay a visit to Bishop Loftus."

"*Ach*, Joel, don't. Not while you're so angry."

"I'm not so much angry as I am clear. I'll be back."

Martha watched him go and began to pray that *Gott* would be glorified in Joel's life.

Joel didn't knock when he entered the bishop's home. The older man was in the kitchen, spreading brown mustard over a slice of bread with a serrated knife.

"Joel Umble—a strange surprise. Where is your—wife?"

"I will not speak of Martha with you."

"Then what will you speak of?" The bishop went on making lunch.

"There is something about me I have never told you. I have the gift of second sight. Not witchcraft, not a cheat—simply, *Gott* has given me the ability to see—beyond what we can see in the everyday world."

"And?" the bishop asked, clearly bored. "Are

you thinking of taking your show on the road to entertain people with your—sight?"

Joel spoke calmly. "No. I come to tell you of a vision I had some time ago. I saw you dying—in your bed, as you sleep. A crushing pain will fill your chest. Your nose will bleed. You will hear every heartbeat in your ears, but no one will help you. No one can help you but *Gott*, and even in death, you will refuse Him."

Joel turned to go.

"Wait." The older man's voice was sharp and haughty. "Why tell me this?"

Joel smiled faintly. "So that you may prepare. Get your heart ready, if you know where your heart is . . . There will be no more spying, no more threats. Look to your own soul, Bishop. Put your own house in order."

Joel turned and started to whistle as he made his way out the front door, and he never looked back.

# Epilogue

"Easter is a sacred time. A time to be thankful for *Gott* and friends, but especially for love. I don't mean some romanticized type of love." Joel closed his eyes for a moment as he pictured Sebastian. "I mean wholehearted, sold-out, sacrificial love . . . So, I guess that's all, folks. Have a great afternoon!"

Joel caught Stephen's eye from where his formerly shunned friend stood at the back of the room and got a much-appreciated nod of approval.

He was picking up his notes from the preaching when Martha came and threw her arms round him. "That was a blessed message, Joel Umble."

"*Ach*, I hope so . . . I want to give people hope. I want them to be secure in the idea that *Gott* loves them and has a plan for their lives . . ." He drew her close and kissed her. "Are you with me in this?"

She returned his kiss with a fervor not meant for the rest of the Ice Mountain community to see, but the backless benches were fortunately empty now. "I'm always with you, Joel Umble."

He laughed in joy. "Well, do you want to *geh* out and roll Easter eggs?"

She gave him an arch look. "If we must, though

that would be perhaps my second choice right now."

He laughed again and took her hand. "Eggs first."

Martha smiled, and they went out together into the spring and sunshine and the pastel hues of new life.

## Center Point Large Print

600 Brooks Road / PO Box 1
Thorndike, ME 04986-0001 USA

**(207) 568-3717**

**US & Canada:**
**1 800 929-9108**
www.centerpointlargeprint.com